"OUR UNFINISHED END"
Written by Jameson Flynn
Edited by Dara Schechter

Our Unfinished End, is a work of fiction based on real people, actual places and historical events.

Copyright Jameson Flynn/Shiloh Press
January 2019
First Edition Published June 2019

Special Thanks :
Page Layout --Francois Granger CREAPRINT
Cover Design-- Olivia Shiloh
Online Editor-- Rachel Simone
Contributing Editor—Susan O'Grady

ISBN 978-0-9738149-5-8

For them that was and those to come...JF

OUR UNFINISHED END

OUR UNFINISHED
END
BY
JAMESON FLYNN

We all live in different worlds, no two journeys be quite the same. Trick is, keep your world small in the universe large.
—*Old Man Miller*

FIRST LIGHT

Some people say they can remember all the way back to when they were babies, even to being in the womb, floating around inside mommy sucking on that umbilical cord. That can't be true. My very first memory is when I was almost four, laying on the grass out in our backyard throwing rotten apples up at the sun, trying to hit it. I wasn't a very bright kid, but I do remember heaving things at the sun made me feel happy. That first day, I'd been throwing all morning and I was running out of apples, just as I was coming close to hitting the sun.

Then I remember our next-door neighbor, Mrs. DiGeorgino, started calling my name, "Jimmy, come in for lunch now. Your sandwich is ready, Jimmy."

I was pretty hungry from all the throwing I'd been doing that morning, but I knew my mom would be mad at me if I went next door and ate lunch with Mrs. DiGeorgino without asking first.

"Jimmy, where are you? Time to come in for lunch now." Mrs. DiGeorgino sounded a little mad that I wasn't coming over right away.

"I'm over here, Mrs. DiGeorgino, over here in my backyard. My mom is already making lunch for me. I can't come over today, maybe tomorrow."

Mrs. DiGeorgino looked over the fence at me but kept insisting I come over for lunch right now.

"Jimmy, if you're not at the table in one minute, then lunchtime is over and no cookies for dessert."

Now I was really getting worried, as lunchtime was already my favorite time of the day and I loved cookies. I put my apples back on the pile, got up and started walking toward Mrs. DiGeorgino who was standing at her backdoor still yelling for Jimmy. Suddenly, another little boy jumped down from their apple tree and ran past Mrs. DiGeorgino into the house.

"Make sure you wash your hands first, Jimmy, and next time come right away when I call you."

Mrs. DiGeorgino looked over, made a funny face at me, shook her head and closed the door. I started crying, I couldn't believe what had just happened. There was another little boy named Jimmy and he lived right next door. I thought I was the only boy named Jimmy in the whole wide world.

I remember looking across the street at the old man sitting on his porch. That was the first day I ever noticed him, but every day after that he was always sitting outside watching the neighborhood. No matter how early I woke up and started playing in the backyard or how late I went inside for dinner, there was Mr. Miller, sitting in his rocking chair on the front porch, reading his newspaper and waving to everyone who walked by. That first day, he smiled and waved at me as I ran inside crying to tell my Mom what had just happened with Mrs. DiGeorgino.

I burst into the kitchen where my mom always was busy cooking something.

"Mommy, mommy, there's another boy named Jimmy and he lives right next door to us. How can that be, Mommy? I thought I was the only Jimmy."

My mother was listening to men talking on the radio. She was crying like me so I thought she must have already known about that other boy. But when she turned up the radio and kept listening to the men arguing, she suddenly stopped crying and started shouting at the radio…

2

"You tell him, Mr. Welch, you tell that McCarthy bum we're not going to tolerate him anymore. He's not fooling anyone. You show him up for the bully he is."

It wasn't until many years later, my sophomore year studying U.S. History at Roma High School, that I figured out why my mom was yelling at the radio that sweltering hot day in June of 1954.

That was the day of the famous exchange between the Army's lawyer, Joseph Welch, who was defending a young associate lawyer at his Boston law firm named Fred Fisher, and Senator Joseph McCarthy who was trying to add Fisher to the blacklist of people considered dangerous and unemployable because of their supposed connections to the Communist party. It was one thing said in their exchange that made all the difference in ending the witch hunt for communists that McCarthy had ignited and stoked throughout the country to the point where families, friends and neighbors were whispering and pointing fingers, accusing those "outsiders" of being communists.

When Mr. Welch responded in the moment to Senator McCarthy's character assassination of Fred Fisher by saying …"At long last, have you no sense of decency sir?"…the audience inside the senate hearing erupted into thunderous applause, heard well outside the room, beyond the nation's capitol building and throughout the entire country, thanks to the live broadcast of the hearings by radio and television stations. From that day on, Republican Senator Joseph McCarthy of Wisconsin and his gang of bullies were discredited, never to be taken seriously again. Soon after, McCarthy's hearings ended abruptly and he was censored by the Senate for making false accusations.

Just a few years later, Joseph McCarthy died of hepatitis in a forgotten military hospital at the age of forty-eight alone, disgraced and destitute with many rumors and accusations being whispered about the true cause of his death. I guess what goes around truly does come around, eventually.

I remember my mother jumping up and down after that exchange. She picked me up and we danced across the kitchen, into our living room and through the dining room, before she put me down and hugged me tight.

"We can't be bullied and we can't be fooled, Jimmy. That's the country we live in. The good people will always win, sometimes it just takes a little while. Sometimes more than a little while."

"But Mom, you said I was the only Jimmy in this world. There's another one living right next door."

"What? Is that why you're crying? I said you were my Jimmy, the only Jimmy in the whole wide world for me. There is no other Jimmy like you, I promise you that."

I stopped throwing rotten apples at the sun after that day and started throwing them at the boy next door, Jimmy DiGeorgino, after he threw three at me. He was five and I was almost four, so our aim wasn't very good. We rarely even hit each other. But we'd get outside extra early every morning just to collect piles of rotten, brown, wet, worm-filled apples that we would heave over the fence using garbage can covers as our shields. Around noon, we would break for lunch when our moms called for us. Then, we'd come back outside rejuvenated from our peanut butter and jelly sandwiches to resume our apple war. Old Man Miller was always watching us, enjoying the show from his front-porch rocking chair across the street.

I never did speak to the other Jimmy that whole

summer, we just threw rotten apples at each other. One day in early September he wasn't in his backyard anymore. My mom said he had started school and would be there every day, except for weekends. I missed that other Jimmy. I guess you could say that little boy next door was my first friend; that's my first memory. The womb? I find that very hard to believe.

Excerpt from live radio broadcast of the Army-McCarthy hearings, June 9th, 1954

MR. WELCH:...And so, Senator, I asked him to go back to Boston. Little did I dream you could be so reckless and so cruel as to do an injury to that lad. It is true he is still with Hale & Dorr. It is true that he will continue to be with Hale & Dorr. It is, I regret to say, equally true that I fear he shall always bear a scar needlessly inflicted by you. If it were in my power to forgive you for your reckless cruelty, I would do so. I like to think I'm a gentle man, but your forgiveness will have to come from someone other than me.

SENATOR McCARTHY: Mr. Chairman? May I say that Mr. Welch talks about this being cruel and reckless. He was just baiting—He was baiting Mr. Cohn for hours, requesting that Mr. Cohn, before sundown, get out of the government anyone who is serving the Communist cause. Now, I just give this man's record and I want to say, Mr. Welch, it has been labeled long before he became a member, as early as 1944...

MR. WELCH: Senator

SENATOR McCARTHY: Let—let me finish.

MR. WELCH: May we not drop this?

SENATOR McCARTHY: Let me finish.

MR. WELCH: We know he belonged to the Lawyer's Guild.

SENATOR McCARTHY: No, let me finish...

MR. WELCH: And Mr. Cohn nods his head at me. I did you, I think, no personal injury, Mr. Cohn?

MR. COHN: No, sir.

MR. WELCH: I meant to do you no personal injury.

MR. COHN: No, sir.

MR. WELCH: And if I did...

SENATOR McCARTHY: No...

MR. WELCH: I beg your pardon. Let us not assassinate this lad further, Senator.

SENATOR McCARTHY: Let's, let's...

MR. WELCH: You've done enough. Have you no sense of decency, sir, at long last? Have you left no sense of decency? (SENATE ROOM ERUPTS IN APPLAUSE)

(Senator Joseph McCarthy died three years later on May 2nd, 1957 at the age of 48. His death certificate listed cause of death as Acute Hepatitis, cause unknown.)

PAPERBOY DELIVERS...The Bad News

If you ever want to really know what's going on behind those closed front doors in any neighborhood, just ask the paperboy. We know and see it all. I've been working this route for two years now, since I turned twelve. Usually by this time on a Friday night I'm already home, eating dinner in front of the television watching my favorite shows. Today is different. Everything changed today, and not for the better.

They told us at school what had happened, even sent us home a little early. But when Kenny Koogan, my boss who manages the circulation for Roma's daily newspaper, showed up at three o'clock with no newspapers in his station wagon, I understood just how strange this day was gonna be. For the first time in my two years of newspaper experience, The Roma Gazette was going to be arriving after dinner.

"Where's my papers, Kenny?"

"They're going to be a little late tonight Wally...we're doing a special late edition because of what happened. Meet me back here at six and I'll have your papers."

Usually Kenny's like a clock, right down to the minute. At three o'clock sharp every weekday, you can hear Kenny's old station wagon putting up the hill, rounding the corner and screeching to a halt on our corner just long enough to toss out the sixty papers for my route. Then, he disappears down the hill to drop off papers to the other five delivery boys in Roma. I'm Kenny's first stop and I have the shortest route, which means I'm always the first one done. Ordinarily, I have just enough time to get home from school, eat a sandwich with some chocolate milk, and still get to the corner in time to meet

Kenny by three. Then I fold and rubberband the papers, load up my bicycle, and deliver to my three neighborhoods, ending with the cul-de-sac where I live on Miller's End. I'm normally done by about four-thirty, but today killed everything that used to be normal, even time. Here it is seven o'clock at night and I'm still out delivering these late-edition Roma Gazettes in a November snow squall just six days before Thanksgiving. Doesn't seem right what happened, nothing seems right.

"Sorry I'm so late tonight, Mrs. MacDonald. It's a special edition because of the shooting."

"Oh, it's a terrible, terrible day, Wally. We heard what happened on the radio but they didn't say very much. Let me get your money. I'll be right back."

"No need, Mrs. MacDonald, I'll collect next week. People shouldn't have to pay for anything today. The news is too sad."

Mrs. MacDonald hugs me tight around my neck. "You're a good boy, Wally Wagner. Don't worry, we'll get through this and things will be better again. Such a horrible thing they did, so much hatred. What has happened to our country, Wally?" She kisses my forehead and closes her door. I can hear her weeping inside as I walk away.

Friday is usually my collection day, when I knock on all the doors to collect money owed for their two weeks of newspaper delivery. It's a nice way to end the week with most folks in a good mood, ready to read their Gazette and relax into the weekend. I usually get tips and even some fresh baked cookies along with the five dollars they owe me. But tonight, I am knocking out of respect, not to collect any money. Tonight, I am delivering the bad news; people need to read about the gunshots heard around the world.

8

We're a small town, so everyone knows everyone else in Roma. I know all the kids who open the doors when I knock, and they know me. "Mom, Wally Wagner's here to collect," says Paula Penders, a sixth grader who is friends with my younger sister. Mrs. Penders, who works at the school in the front office, comes to the door in her bathrobe drinking a glass of red wine. Her eyes are glassy and wet but I can see she is trying not to cry in front of me.

"Thank you, Wally, for stopping by. I thought there might not be a paper today with what happened. He was such a beautiful man, and his wife, how will she be able to move on? It just doesn't make any sense. We're supposed to be better than this." She hands me a ten-dollar bill and tells me to keep the change.

"No, Mrs. Penders, I'm not collecting today. I don't think it's right. This day is too important for money."

I hand her back the ten dollars and she breaks down into tears, dropping her wine glass to the floor. Little Paula Penders starts crying too, not understanding why but because her mother is in tears she joins in. I want to say something, anything to make them feel better, but there are no words in me. The storm is getting worse. I have to finish my route.

Halfway up the Mountain Road, I turn the corner at Miller's End to make my first stop at the Gallo's house. Mr. Gallo opens the door, still dressed in his policeman's uniform. He's a big man with a red scar running down his left cheek from when he fought in World War II against the Japanese. Most of the kids in Roma are afraid of Mr. Gallo, but I'm not, he's always been nice to me.

"Delivering the Gazette in a snowstorm...you're like the Pony Express, Wally. The newspaper must go through. You got change for a twenty?"

"Not tonight, Mr. Gallo. I'm just delivering the special late edition so everyone has the news about what happened today. I'll collect next week sir, not today."

"It was bound to happen, Wally. He pissed off too many people in power. Too many Protestants, that's for sure. He was the first, hell, he was the only Catholic president we've ever had and look what they did to him. Whoever says this isn't a Protestant country just isn't paying attention. Everything's going to change from here on. Everyone's going to be afraid again. It doesn't really matter who pulled the trigger. It matters more who got him to do it. Thanks for doing your duty, Wally, you're a good kid. Now get on home before this storm gets any worse."

Mr. Gallo salutes me as I get on my bicycle. As I ride away, I can still see him standing in his doorway looking up at the night sky as if he's searching for something.

I should already be home all warm and cozy by now, figuring out what I want to eat for dessert. But today, I mean tonight, I feel it's important to get these special-edition newspapers delivered to my customers, my neighbors, my friends who are in shock and despair over what happened in Dallas today. I wonder if Mr. Gallo is right, that everyone will be afraid from now on. Afraid of what?

The snow is falling heavier now with the wind whipping at my back, pushing me homeward. There are ten houses on my street, each set on one acre of land. This neighborhood used to be part of the south section of Miller's Farm. The Millers are one of Roma's oldest families who used this section of land to feed and shelter their horses, cows and pigs. About thirty years ago one of the Miller descendants decided to sell the farm and all the land to a developer who wanted to build one hundred homes on the mountain's south slope. My parents bought one of the ten homes that finally did get built on this quiet dead end street called, Miller's End.

Working my way along our street, I pedal my bicycle up the long driveways and past the spacious yards of our neighbors. Tonight, it feels like everyone has been waiting for me as they quickly open their doors to my knock. Next stop is the Stringers where little Sammy opens the door in his pajamas. Is it that late already? Sammy shows me the new model airplane he put together with his older brother, Sonny. As I turn to leave, Sammy scoops up some snow from the porch and throws a snowball at me. The kid has no idea what happened today, which is good because he will never have to know the sadness everyone else is feeling. I'm happy for Sammy Stringer and his innocence, even though his snowball hits me in the neck and runs down my back, getting me all wet. Pretty nice throw for a little kid, I have to admit that.

Old Man Miller is sitting on his front porch just like always, keeping watch on the neighborhood even in this snowstorm.

"They got him, I knew they would. Country wasn't ready for so much change. We are a capitalist country where the capitalists, the rich folk, run things, not the President. He works for them. He must have told all those Mayflower blue bloods to go to hell, so they sent him first. You're going to remember this day your whole life, Wally...Friday, November 22nd, 1963. I guarantee you that. Now, why is my paper so damn late?"

"Special-edition, Mr. Miller. We had to wait for the official story to come out before we could print the news. I haven't even had dinner yet."

"You got that right, Wally. I'm sure they had to make up an official story. A lone gunman, how did they know that right away? You get on home now and enjoy your dinner. This storm's gonna be a whopper. I can always tell. I remember back in 1863, it snowed for seven days straight, killed all the cows…"

"Good night, Mr. Miller."

Mr. Miller's always got stories that go way back, and he'll keep telling them whether I'm there or not. I don't know exactly how old he is; nobody around here does since he was already living in this neighborhood long before anyone else who lives here now. My mom says he came with the house, so we just accept Mr. Miller as that crazy old man who sits on his front porch watching everyone go by.

Next, I deliver to my friend Jimmy Jackman's house. It's just Jimmy and his mother living in their house across from Mr. Miller. They don't have a television yet, so Jimmy listens to the radio a lot and plays his guitar along with the songs. He's getting pretty good.

"Hey, Jimmy. I'm just dropping off your paper. No collection today because of what happened.

How's your mom?"

"My mom's pretty broken up, Wally. She voted for him, thought he was gonna make everything better. She's had the radio on and been crying ever since I got home from school. I think the newspaper stories are going to make her even sadder. Maybe I won't give it to her until tomorrow. What do you think, Wally, is that a good idea?"

"I don't know, Jimmy, I'm too cold to know anything right now. She might get mad since you don't have a TV. But at least now she has the late edition. Probably you should give it

12

to her. It might just stop her from crying. I don't think you can cry and read at the same time."

"Thanks, Wally. You're probably right, at least it will get her away from the radio. I'll see you tomorrow. Maybe we'll throw the football around."

"See you tomorrow, Jimmy. Take care of your mom and let us know if you need anything."

I feel bad for Jimmy Jackman. It's always been just him and his mom ever since they moved here when he was a little kid, not even in school yet. Jimmy's the man of his house and he's not even fourteen yet. Tonight, he has to take care of his mom. That doesn't seem fair to Jimmy.

The last stop before my house is always the DiGeorgino's where the other Jimmy lives. I'm friends with both the Jimmies, but they never do seem to get along, even though they live right next door to each other. No matter what sport or game we're playing, the Jimmies are always on opposite sides, going at it like it's a private war between them. The DiGeorgino house is dark except for the light from the television set in their living room. I knock but nobody answers. I knock again, this time louder, and hear footsteps coming to the door.

"Oh, Wally, it's you. I thought there might not be a newspaper today with everything that's happened. You're out so late. Oh, you must be freezing in this snowstorm. We're watching the news on television. Walter Cronkite is so choked up he can hardly speak. Jimmy, Jimmy, where are you? Wally's here with the newspaper. I'll go get your money, Wally, just wait a minute. Come in out of the cold."

"No thanks, Mr. DiGeorgino, I really need to get home and have dinner with my family. I'm not collecting today. I just wanted to make sure you got your newspaper so you can read all about what happened. Tell Jimmy I'll see him tomorrow. We'll play some football in the snow. Goodnight now."

"Goodnight, Wally and thank you. Jimmy, Wally says he'll see you tomorrow. What are you doing up there? Come down and watch Walter Cronkite with me. He's crying."

As I push my bicycle across the street to my house, I turn around to see Jimmy DiGeorgino up on his roof smoking a cigarette. I wave, but he doesn't wave back; he's too busy scampering inside his bedroom window to the approaching voice of Mrs. DiGeorgino asking, "Jimmy, where are you Jimmy?"

I can smell my mom's spaghetti sauce the moment I walk through our front door. Friday night is always spaghetti and meatballs at the Wagners. Why should tonight be any different? My little sister, Ava, meets me at the front door and hugs me tight.

"Wally, I'm so glad you're home. It's all so sad."

Ava takes my hand and leads me into the living room where my mom and dad are watching Walter Cronkite on the CBS news report talk about the lone gunman who shot our President John F. Kennedy during a parade in Dallas, Texas. My parents are sitting on the floor in front of our fireplace holding each other as they weep. It is the first time I have ever seen my father cry. Over the next few days, it will not be the last. Ava and I squeeze hands and kneel down to join our parents in this moment of grief that will never leave our memories in the many years to come. I can grieve now, my duty is done. I have delivered the bad news that needed to be reported. I am at home with the people I love, with my family who love me back. Tomorrow, I will wake up and throw the football with my friends. I will move forward in my life. But everything will be different from now on, I am sure of that...

WALTER CRONKITE: ...President Kennedy was assassinated by a lone gunman in Dallas, Texas. He died at 1PM Central Standard Time, 2 o'clock Eastern Standard Time today, Friday, November 22nd 1963, a day that will be long remembered. Vice President Lyndon Johnson has left the hospital in Dallas but we do not know where he has proceeded. Presumably, he will be taking the oath of office shortly and become the 36th President of the United States...The world's doubts must be put to rest about what happened today. Tonight there will be few Americans who will go to bed without carrying with them the sense that somehow they have failed. If in the search of our conscience we find a new dedication to the American concepts that brook no political, sectional, religious or racial divisions, then maybe it will be possible to say that John Fitzgerald Kennedy did not die in vain...
This is Walter Cronkite, good night America.

A few days later my dad sold our burgundy Pontiac convertible with the sporty white-wall tires and bought a boring black Ford station wagon. I loved that convertible, I knew he did too.

When I asked my dad why he sold our Pontiac, he told me, "It's just safer to fit in than to stand out, Wally."

I understood then what Mr. Gallo meant when he said that everyone would be afraid from now on.

BOY NEXT DOOR

I hate him. Of all the places in the world to live, I can't believe it has to be right next door to us. Ever since I found out about them, I've done everything I can to hurt him and make them move out, but nothing has worked. He never even seems to notice. That makes me hate him and his mother even more. How can they not notice me? How could my dad do this to us, to my mom?

I used to watch him from the tree in my backyard. He was always a weird little kid who spent his days throwing apples and acorns up at the sun. Who does that? Then I started throwing rotten apples at him, and he threw them back. What he didn't know, because I never actually hit him, I was loading my rotten apples with rocks stuffed inside. If only I had better aim and a better arm, that would have been the end of little Jimmy Jackman right then and there, and maybe my mom would have stopped crying all the time.

I remember the night my dad left us. He was arguing so loud with my mom, they woke me up. It was after midnight. I crept to the top of the staircase and watched them fight. My mom was crying and throwing things at my dad. She kept saying, "How could you? How could you do this to us?"

He was standing by the front door with his coat on and two suitcases all packed up. "It just happened, Grace. These things just happen. We grew up together in the old neighborhood in Brooklyn. I've known her since the first grade."

"So you had to move her here, with the kid?"

"No, I told her not to, but she came here anyway. How

could I stop her?"

"Right next door to us, and his name is Jimmy? What the hell is the matter with you?"

"I didn't name him, she just always knew I liked that name. I think she might be a little crazy."

"You think she's crazy, what about you? Big Dominick DeGeorgino, Roma's trusty milkman, delivering his milk to all the lonely women for miles around. It's a small town, you idiot. Don't you think people talk and whisper and point? That's all they do. You've embarrassed me, and even worse, you've made a joke of our family. I want you out Dominick, tonight. I want you to leave Roma and never come back. Your bags are packed, you're all ready to go. Just leave, we're better off without you. I never want to see you again."

I never did see my dad again after that night. He picked up those two suitcases, muttered something about being sorry and walked out the door. At breakfast the next morning, it was just me and my mom; she was still crying but trying not to. Mom told me dad had moved out and it would just be the two of us from now on. That's what happens to families sometimes, she said.

I was only five but I already knew that my mom would always be sad, all because of that little idiot boy living next door with his crazy mother. Everything was his fault, and I was going to make him pay for it. That was the day I started throwing rotten rock apples at his head.

When that didn't work I tried other stuff. I filled up the front tire on his bicycle with too much air so it would explode and cause a crash when he was riding fast down the mountain road. It never did explode, no matter how much air I pumped in. Two summers later I challenged him to a tree-climbing contest to see who could climb the highest. I put him on the side with all the dead branches, hoping he would reach for one too far out and too weak to hold, making him fall out of the tree from way up top. Instead, he climbed like a monkey, jumping from branch to branch like he was in a Tarzan movie. I ended up falling that day from thirty feet up, breaking both of my arms and cracking three ribs. Again, all of my pain and suffering was caused by that little goon living next door to us. He had to go.

Time after time, everything I did to hurt him, or even better, kill him, never left a scratch on him. When we played football in the neighborhood, I would always tackle him extra hard, even if we were just playing touch. He got to be so good at running away from me that by high school he was the fastest player with the best moves on the team. Me? I ended up with two bad knees and shin splints from all my missed flying tackles that turned into crash landings on hard ground, as little Jimmy Jackman pranced his way to another touchdown. I hate that kid...

I can see into his bedroom from up here on our roof. He plays his guitar every night along with his record player, trying to become the next Elvis, or so he can join the Beatles. He'll just sit there for hours practicing chords and making believe he's performing a concert in front of thousands of cheering fans. He even takes bows at the end of songs. Who does that? I don't bow at the end of every song when I practice my tuba, and I'm actually in a band, the Roma Marching Band. We perform at every game, parade and event in town, so I don't need to play make believe in my bedroom. I play my tuba for real people.

It's early April now. Two and a half more months and I'll be graduating from Roma High School, Class of '68. No more school for me. I'm joining the Marines and heading straight over to Vietnam to kick ass and kill some gooks in the name of freedom and liberty, compliments of the red, white and blue. I don't like the idea of leaving my mom alone with that little shit and his mom still living next door. Lately, I've been bringing my .22 rifle up here with me and sighting him through my night-scope. It would be such an easy shot to hit him as he sits there strumming those guitar strings. But just the angle alone would do me in, they'd know it was me and that would be it for going to Nam. I'd be going to jail instead. Nah, if I'm gonna shoot him it has to look like a hunting accident. Problem is, Jimmy Jackman doesn't hunt. Everything I did over the years was always to make it look accidental. I don't want to get blamed, I just want him dead. I feel so good perched up here on my rooftop like a sniper with little Jimmy in my crosshair, knowing that I could pull the trigger and that would be the end of him.

It's all over the news tonight how Martin Luther King was shot by a sniper outside his hotel room in Memphis. That would have been an easy shot too. It happened at about six o'clock and they pronounced him dead by seven. I don't know much about Martin Luther King, just what they told us in school. I know that a lot of black people, and some white people too, looked up to him as a leader. I know he made that "I Have A Dream" speech when they all marched on our nation's capitol in Washington D.C. They never should have let them march. That's why he got shot.

I knew somebody was gonna shoot Martin Luther King. Hell, it didn't take a genius to see that bullet coming. President Kennedy got shot a few years back in '63. Somebody's gonna shoot his brother Robert for sure before they let another Catholic Kennedy become President. Martin Luther King was just as dangerous as those Kennedys with his big dreams about making things better and changing this country into one giant lovefest where everyone is equal. That's not who we are here in the good ole U.S. of A.; we never were and never will be. Why would anyone believe they could change things all these years later?

When we read the Constitution of the United States in history class, I understood "We The People" to mean exactly what it said…We the white, rich, Protestant landowners are the only true people of this country; not the indentured servants, the slaves, the women, or the Indians. They don't count. Hell, they didn't even get to vote until a few years ago. Everybody knows it's never a lone gunman who fires the kill shot. It's We The People, because we stand to lose a whole lot more than anyone else if anything ever really changes and the country does a do-over. I don't even know why people act surprised when these assassinations keep happening. I'm more surprised when they don't.

"Jimmy, Jimmy, come down here and watch the news with me."

"I'm coming Mom, be there in a minute or two."

"Hurry up, Jimmy, they're going to play Martin Luther King's, " I Have A Dream" speech."

"I heard it already in school Mom. None of his dreams are gonna come true."

"Jimmy, you come down here right now and stop being disrespectful to Doctor Martin Luther King."

Where did that little shit go? I can't see him anywhere. Looking through my scope, he's not in his bedroom, not in the living room, not in the kitchen. There he is, in their dining room with his mom. What are they doing on their knees? It looks like they're praying...praying for what? My mom has our T.V. turned up full blast downstairs so I can hear it. It sounds like every other house in our neighborhood is watching too, as Martin Luther King's strong voice reaches beyond their living rooms and fills the night air with the dreams he shared with all those people who marched on Washington in August of 1963, just a few months before John F. Kennedy got shot.

...And so even though we face the difficulties of today and tomorrow, I still have a dream. It is a dream deeply rooted in the American dream...

Well, he's not gonna have any dreams tomorrow, that's for sure. Lone gunman my ass. They'll find some patsy to pin it on, some hillbilly idiot, I'm sure. But he didn't do it alone, if he did it at all. It'll be Oswald all over again.

... I have a Dream that one day this nation will rise up and live out the true meaning of its creed: We hold these truths to be self-evident, that all men are created equal."...

I'm just saying how things really work in this country. That's why I'm joining the Marines soon as I get out of school this June. It's better to be with them than against them if you care about staying alive during hunting season, which is what these last few years have become.

...I have a Dream that one day on the red hills of Georgia, the sons of former slaves and the sons of former slave owners will be able to sit down together at the table of brotherhood...

Because, We The People would rather kill you before we let Life, Liberty and most especially our Pursuit of Happiness be taken away from us. I didn't listen very much in school, but I did hear that message loud and clear.

...I have a Dream that one day even the state of Mississippi, a state sweltering with the heat of injustice, sweltering with the heat of oppression, will be transformed into an oasis of freedom and justice...

It would be so easy to take the shot right now and put an end to little Jimmy and his mom as they kneel there, crying and praying for Martin Luther King. But then I'd be the patsy. His voice sounds stronger now, like it's coming down from the mountaintop, as if Martin Luther King is standing right over me. Someone's playing their TV even louder than the other houses. It's coming from Mr. Miller's house. That crazy old man, he's got his television out there on his front porch and he's staring up at the stars; no wait, what the hell, he's looking right at me. How can he see me up here? How long has he been watching me? Holy shit, I'm slipping down, I'm falling off the roof …

...I Have a Dream that my four little children will one day live in a nation where they will not be judged by the color of their skin but by the content of their character. I Have a Dream today!...

CBS Nightly News Report with Walter Cronkite
April 4th, 1968—

—Good evening...Dr. Martin Luther King, the apostle of non-violence in the civil rights movement has been shot to death in Memphis, Tennessee...Police have issued an All-Points-Bulletin for a well-dressed young man seen running from the scene. Officers also reported chasing and firing on a radio-equipped car containing two white men...

Dr. King was standing on the balcony of his second floor hotel room tonight when a shot was fired from across the street...In a friend's words, the bullet exploded in his face...Police rushed the 39-year old Negro leader to a hospital where he died of a bullet wound to the neck. Martin Luther King was pronounced dead at 7:05 PM on this night, April 4th, 1968...

A week later, they pinned this one on some guy named James Earl Ray, who supposedly confessed, then withdrew his confession. This patsy was caught in London of all places. Two months later, almost to the day, Robert Kennedy was assassinated after winning the California presidential primary in a landslide. According to Walter Cronkite's official story that night, it was the act of yet another lone gunman. The 1960s was a hunting season like no other, to be always remembered and never forgotten by, **We The People.**

FORGET ABOUT IT

"Oh, Daddy, when is it going to happen? We've been waiting for so long and I'm getting really tired. I have to wake up early for camp tomorrow."

"Hold on just a little bit longer, Gumball. They're still getting ready. They have to be really careful so nothing goes wrong. This is a big deal. I know you're tired, but some things are worth waiting for."

"Maybe we should let them go to sleep and wake them up when it's time, Gino. I'll go get some more pillows and comforters so we can make a big floor bed in front of the television. How's that, Gemma?"

"Yes, Mommy, that's what we need. One giant bed for all of us, for you and Daddy too. We can make a tent."

"No, Gemma, we don't need a tent, just some pillows and comforters for padding. I'll bring them down. Theresa, will you help me?"

"Sure Mom, but if they come out while we're upstairs, somebody yell. I want to see them when they open the door. I don't want to miss it."

"It's not even that late, Greta, barely ten o'clock. This is one of those big family moments we have to do together because we're never gonna get another chance like this. It's a once-in-a-lifetime event and the Gallos get to see it together. Hurry up, set up camp. I'll call you if anything happens. Now move out."

"Calm down, Sergeant Gino. I'll make it comfortable and cozy for them so they can nod off if they want. We can wake them when it's time, whenever that is. Look, Gemma's already falling asleep."

"C'mon Gumball, I know you're faking. Your eyes are moving."

"My name's not Gumball, it's Gemma, and I am too really asleep, Daddy. But Ernest and Julio, they're faking. You can tell because they're smiling and moving their lips."

"I'm having a really good dream, that's why I'm smiling. How about you, Ernest?"

"Me too, Julio, a fantastic dream, and now I'm talking in my sleep. Gemma, I'm coming to get you. I am talking to you from outer space."

"See, Daddy, they're not really asleep, just faking it, and trying to scare me like always."

"Greta, where are those pillows? I think something's about to happen."

"I'm not sleepy, Dad, I'm with you. This is the big moment that could change everything. I'm not gonna sleep through it," said Frankie, adjusting the television antenna.

"See, Gemma, your big brother Frankie knows what's what. He's not even tired. The excitement alone should keep you awake."

"I don't think she's faking now, Dad. Gumball's out for the count."

I watch them each close their eyes and fall into a deep sleep as if they flipped an Off switch. Gemma, our youngest, goes out first, followed by her older brothers by two years Ernest and Julio, our twins. They do everything together. Sitting over on the couch glued to the television set is Frankie, our oldest son who already looks so much like me it's scary. Helping my wife spread pillows and comforters over and around our sleeping beauties is their big sister, Theresa, who at twelve is one of those old souls with wisdom well beyond her years. We are the Gallos, all seven of us present and accounted for on this warm July night in Roma.

"Jeez Greta, are you sure they even need any blankets? It's pretty hot tonight."

"You say that every night, Gino, and then the summer breeze blows down from the mountain. I may let them sleep here tonight instead of carrying them upstairs. Theresa, could you put another pillow under Gemma's head?"

I sit back and watch Greta turn our living room into a sleep chamber for the kids. She has a way of making everything warm and cozy, no matter what the situation. I know I'm a lucky man to have found her. Together we made this beautiful family. These are the moments I live for. It's taken a while but I understand now. It is the people you love and who love you back who make your world beautiful. Nothing and no one else matters. We all live in different worlds, I know that now. But it's the people you let into your world who make the difference between beauty and ugly; joy and sorrow; laughter and tears.

"Dad, how many people do you think are watching tonight?"

"Everyone in Roma who has a TV, that's for sure, Frankie. All over the country, I'd bet maybe fifty million people are watching. If you count everyone around the world with television sets sitting up no matter what time it is, I'd say over a hundred million people are watching and waiting for that door to open. Pretty exciting stuff, hey, Frankie?"

I'm in the tail end of my second quarter of life now and happy to have made it this far. Rocco would be proud of me, maybe even a little surprised. Rocco Rendoza was a guy I knew growing up in the Bronx. We were best friends in school, served lots of detention time and survived the nuns together. Then, we joined the Army with the rest of the kids from our neighborhood, to fight the Japanese and the Germans in World War II so there would never be another world war again.

Rocco had this theory about the four stages of life. He explained it to me one night while we hid deep inside a cave waiting for death to find us. According to Rocco, the first quarter is up until the age of twenty-two. That's when your parents make all the big decisions and key choices for you because you're just a kid who doesn't know shit from shinola yet. You are whatever they tell you to be. Rocco called this first quarter the "Tell Me Everything Stage." He divided each quarter of life equally into twenty-two years, give or take a few according to the person. Rocco figured most people didn't make it past the age of eighty-eight, and if you did, you wished you didn't.

Back then, the Army kept you all together when you were from the same neighborhood and signed up at the same time. They figured we were already a unit from all the time we'd spent together growing up in our Bronx neighborhood. Two weeks after we signed the enlistment papers, we were on a bus to North Carolina for six weeks of bootcamp. None of us had ever been anywhere so North Carolina sounded like an exotic paradise. It wasn't. I'd never been so hot or gotten up so early in my life. Rocco said it felt like a gym class that would never end. But six weeks later, we could all shoot guns and were in the best shape of our lives. I lost twenty pounds and Rocco grew two inches. The best part of it was, when our orders came through they stationed our entire unit in the Caribbean. If the Germans decided to sneak attack Florida, the Bronx Boys would be our first line of defense. We couldn't have been

28

happier spending our days and nights drinking Jamaican rum, playing cards, singing calypso and dancing with the locals. It truly was an island paradise for almost three years, until the war ended and everything changed with one simple communication from Washington ordering our unit to deploy to the Philippine Islands for what they called cleanup duty. It didn't sound so bad, those simple pieces of paper never do. We figured we'd be cleaning up debris and rebuilding bridges knocked out during the naval battle of Leyte, followed by our invasion of the islands that pushed the Japanese out of the Philippines in October of 1944. But this was almost a year later. The atom bombs had already been dropped on Hiroshima and Nagasaki, decimating the cities and killing more than 250,000 people, mostly citizens. The Japanese had surrendered in August of 1945, and our tour was almost up. We were all getting ready to head back home and celebrate our victory, even though we didn't have much to do with it. Then came our new orders.

"Dad, did you hear that, they're getting ready to open the hatch. Should I wake them?"

"Let's give it a minute, Frankie. Sometimes it takes a while to make it happen when you're dealing with chains of command. Soon as the door actually opens, we'll wake them up. How are you doing, Theresa? What is it, about ten-fifteen? Won't be long now."

"I'm fine, Dad. I usually read in bed until midnight so this is still early for me. I don't think Frankie's going to be able to sleep for a week after this."

"Sleep is overrated, Theresa. Being wide awake when it matters most, that's what's important. Right, Dad?"

"Greta, our kids are philosophers. I should be writing

this stuff down."

"They get it from you, Gino, the oracle of Roma."

Rocco's second quarter of life goes from twenty-two to forty-four years old, which is where I'm at now. This is after you have left home, you're not living with or being controlled by your parents anymore. You're making your own choices and defining who you want to be as your own person. Some people get married, like me and Greta did, some stay single, but in Rocco's theory, it's you alone who makes the choices here, nobody else. Rocco called this second quarter the "All About You" stage.

When we arrived in the Philippines on the island of Luzon we found out exactly what cleanup duty meant. To our horror, we were assigned to clean out the caves where the last of the hardened Japanese jungle soldiers were hiding and still fighting, refusing to surrender even after they'd been told the war was over and Japan had lost. I was a sergeant by now, and Rocco was my corporal. It was up to us to lead our unit, our neighborhood friends, deep into Luzon's dark cavernous caves armed with machine guns, grenades and flamethrowers to force out what was left of the feared Japanese jungle fighters.

Rocco's third quarter, the one I'm about to enter, is when all the choices you have made come home to roost. By now, you're forty-four to sixty-six in the "You Are Who You Are" stage.

Whether you got married, divorced, stayed single, became a drug addict, did some time, or just stayed clean and sober, whatever direction your life took, it's all on you now. By third quarter, it was clear who you were as a person; you were defined by the choices you made and actions you took, or didn't take. Rocco believed for many people, this was the toughest quarter of life because all hope is lost for things getting any better. From here on—"You Are Who You Are."

"Wake them up Frankie, they're opening the hatch. Theresa, you shake Gemma. Frankie, tell Ernest and Julio it's time. Oh this is gonna be amazing. Hold my hand, Greta, we're doing this together, like everything else."

It was the very first cave they sent us into on that rainy Friday morning when everything went horribly wrong. We were barely a half hour into the cave when one by one my men started falling from gunfire and bayonets that came at us out of the pitch-black darkness.

Eight hours later, we had gone from a unit of fourteen men down to just the two of us, Rocco and me. We'd watched our boyhood friends suffer horrible deaths, killed by a war that had ended almost two months ago but refused to stop taking lives.

By now, we'd climbed to the highest ground we could find, hiding behind boulders to wait for the dawn and hopefully some light to guide us out of the cave. This is when Rocco decided to explain his theory of life to me to help us both stay awake through this longest nightmare of a night, which we both thought might be our last. The final stage, Corporal Rocco Rendoza's fourth quarter, was what he called the "Spectator In Life" period." By now you're old, if you made it that far, from age sixty-six to eighty-eight. Anything after eighty-eight, Rocco said, was pure gravy. In this stage, you're just watching everyone else live their lives, maybe enjoying some grandchildren and great-grandchildren. But your movie is over; you're just an extra now, waiting for the final credits to roll so you can fade to black. Spectator stage is a great time if you lived a good life, or it could be a never ending horror show if you've been a fucking asshole or a two-faced bitch your whole life. Rocco said for many people, the fourth quarter was not a very good time.

Just as Rocco finished whispering to me his fourth quarter "Spectator In Life" finale, a rock came crashing down from the darkness above us, caving in Rocco Rendoza's skull. I looked up just in time to see what looked like a demon but was really a scraggly-bearded, naked Japanese soldier flying in mid-air, coming down on me with a bayonet in each hand. He landed on top of me with the full force of an anchor being dropped, dragging one of his bayonets down my face as he hit me. That's how I got this red scar that runs from my forehead to my chin and scares all the kids in Roma, all of them except mine who never seem to notice it. My kids just see their dad Gino, their hero, their best friend and biggest fan. I guess love truly is blind.

I never was much of a fighter, probably more of a momma's boy. But in that moment, I could hear my mother's voice loud and clear telling me to come home. From the last time I saw her when I left for bootcamp to the last line in every letter she wrote me, it was always the same voice so strong and clear saying, "Come home to me, Gino."

He raised both bayonets above his head and screamed something in Japanese as I grabbed for the bloody rock that had killed my friend Rocco Rendozza. I smashed the side of his head in and he fell off of me. He still had the bayonets and was trying to get to his feet so I smashed his head again, and again and again until his skull cracked open and he stopped moving. I took his bayonets, and from that moment on I can only remember moving forward in the darkness, flailing the long blades and crying out, "I'm coming home Momma, I'm coming home to you."

A few hours later, just up ahead I saw the tiniest ray of light, my beacon of hope. When I finally made it to that light I met the reinforcement platoon we had radioed for twelve hours earlier. They had decided not to enter the cave under darkness and instead waited for daylight to come. The doctors told me later that I was covered in blood, my body riddled with multiple bullet and stab wounds; but I was still swinging those two bloody bayonets when the platoon reached me. Searching further inside the cave, they found the bodies of my Bronx Boys platoon, along with five dead Japanese soldiers, four mutilated by bayonet and one laying naked with his skull bashed in. I was awarded the Silver Star, a Purple Heart and best of all, an Honorable Discharge. Three months later, I was getting off the train at Grand Central Station hugging my mother who just kept saying, "You came home to me, Gino, my baby boy came home to me."

"Funny, how I think back to that cave in the Philippines tonight, of all nights. I haven't thought about it in years. My motto about the bad parts and the bad people in life is to just Forget About It. You don't have to forgive, just forget and move forward. That way, you can sleep at night just like an innocent kid, instead of remembering all the bad stuff all the time…Forget About It.

"It's happening, there he is stepping down. You see him, Gemma? Ernest, Julio, take that blanket off your heads and look at what's happening right now about two-hundred and fifty thousand miles right up above Roma."

Some of the best moments in life come out of the worst moments ever. Turns out I met my beautiful wife, Greta, at the hospital they sent me to in Hawaii. She was my nurse, and from the very first day we met, she never cared about my scar. Greta just liked how I made her laugh. So, I spent the next three months making Greta laugh, and by the time I left for home, we were engaged. Now, all these years later, we have these amazing kids so full of hope and wonder, and I have a beautiful life I never could have even imagined without Greta.

"This is it, kids. This is when everything changes and all things become possible. Tonight, we're to the moon, on the moon, over the moon..."

SUNDAY JULY 20TH, 1969 NBC NEWS
—Astronaut Neil Armstrong has stepped off the Eagle's footpad and on to the moon's surface—
"The Eagle has landed...That's one small step for man, one giant leap for mankind"

Gemma runs over to the window and looks up at the moon. "Oh Daddy, there really is a man on the moon tonight. I can see him."

"Me too, Gemma, I can see him too."

BAT IN THE BELFRY

"No batter, no batter, no batter. Sammy can't hit, that bat's too big for him. Smoke him, Satchmo. Give him the cloud ball."

Why me? Why am I always the last out? Then everyone's gonna say tomorrow in school that I lost the game. If Coach Callahan would just play me earlier, then I wouldn't always be batting in the last inning for the final out. It just doesn't seem fair to me.

"Put it down the middle, Satchmo. He's not even gonna swing."

"Strike one," yells the umpire.

"I wasn't even ready, Ump. Is Conrad allowed to talk like that? It's really distracting when I'm trying to concentrate on hitting the ball. He's insulting me too, saying my bat is too big for me. Is he allowed to do that? It doesn't seem very sportsmanlike."

"Yes, Sammy, he can talk all he wants, so long as he doesn't curse or use racial slurs. I agree, it's not very nice but some catchers do it anyway. It is annoying to me too, but that's why they do it. Just take your swings and let's head on home. Now let's play ball and get this game over with before it gets too dark."

We're down 4-3 with two outs already. The bases are loaded and we're in the last inning, playing against the undefeated Babylon Wasps. They were last year's champions. Even my own teammates were telling Coach Callahan to pinch hit for me so we can win this game. That hurts my feelings. If I could just get on base, a run will score and I'll be off the hook.

Coach Callahan's son, Patrick, can make the last out. The game will be all tied up 4-4 and maybe the umpire will have to end it for getting too dark. All I have to do is take my swing and maybe something good will happen. My big brother, Sonny, had lots of game-winning hits when he played for Roma. He always tells me, if you don't take your swing, Sammy, nothing good is ever gonna happen. Sonny's in the Marines over in Vietnam now, but he still writes to me every week asking how many home runs I have. So far this season, or any season, it's been Zilch. But I keep swinging the big Mickey Mantle bat he gave me before he left to join the Marines.

"Okay, Satchmo, bring the smoker, right down the middle. Time to send these clowns home for beddy-by."

Just because the Wasps are in first place doesn't give them the right to talk so mean. Their pitcher laughs at me as he winds up to throw his fastball right down the middle like their big-mouthed catcher, Conrad, told him to do. I see the ball leave his hand, watch it become Conrad's trash-talking head as it insults its way toward me. I hate that fat, ugly head and swing my Mickey Mantle bat as hard as I can right at it.

"No batter, no batter, no...what the hell?"

With a loud crack, the ball ricochets off my bat, down the third base line into the outfield and rolls all the way to the fence. I stand there frozen in the batter's box between the now mute Conrad and Mr. Umpire, both in shock and lost in disbelief at what just happened. Jimmy Blake, who was on third, comes running home to score the first run, tying the game at 4-4.

Jimmy pushes me toward first base and says, "You better start running, Sammy, or they're gonna get you out."

Just as I take off running, Peter Proctor crosses home

36

plate for our second run to make the score 5-4. With that run, the game should be over but everyone is still playing, even the umpire, who calls Casey Caldwell safe for another run, as I reach second base and head for third. Rounding third base and heading for home, I hear Coach Callahan, my entire team and everyone in our stands telling me to go back to third base. Up ahead, I see why. Conrad, the Wasp's oversized catcher, is waiting for me at home plate and he already has the ball in his hand. Even worse, he's laughing at me. It's too late to turn back, I'm already half-way to home. I lower my head like a little bull and run my fastest straight toward home plate with only Conrad the trash-talker standing between me and my grand slam. I know this is gonna hurt. He's bigger, heavier and two grades ahead of me, three if you count him being left back. But like my big brother, Sonny, told me, "You gotta take your swing, Sammy, or nothing's ever gonna happen." I plow into Conrad and the umpire standing behind him, sending us all up into the air then landing us in a cloud of dust. I spit dirt out of my mouth and look over to see Conrad sprawled on top of the umpire a few feet away. I'm sitting directly on top of home plate staring at the baseball sitting in front of me on the grass. I look over to the umpire and point to the ball.

Mr. Umpire pushes Conrad off of him and says, "Safe, game over; it's a grand slam. Final score 7-4, Roma wins."

Both teams come running out, mine to celebrate and lift me up onto their shoulders; the Wasps to complain that I should be out and none of the runs should count, even though Conrad dropped the ball. The umpire holds his ground, tells them they're wrong and the game is over. Final score 7-4, we win. Suddenly all my teammates love me. Even Coach Callahan gives me a hug. We beat the Babylon Wasps, the best team in the league, and last year's champions. I hit the game winner, a grand-slam even. I can't wait to get home and tell my mom. Wait till Sonny gets my next letter telling him about my grand slam. He'll be so proud of his little brother.

Riding my bike home, I have to make one quick stop. But I want to get home in time for the big game on television. I think he's gonna do it tonight and I want to see it happen. First though, I have to clang the golden bell. Sonny taught me about this Roma tradition…whenever your touchdown, or basket, or home run, or goal makes the difference to win the game, you have to climb the belfry steps in town hall and ring the golden bell to make sure it happens again. My big brother, Sonny, got to ring it lots of times when he played for Roma. He was great at every sport. Today is my turn to ring the golden bell for the very first time. I hide my bike behind the hedges, sneak in through the side door and climb the old winding staircase up the belfry. It's almost seven o'clock so Town Hall is empty. Everyone's already gone home for dinner and to watch the big game. I carry my Mickey Mantle bat up with me to push the bell and get it clanging. It has to clang ten times to make it count and guarantee more game-winners. Then, I have to get out of there without getting caught. Sonny never got caught.

I climb the dark, narrow stairway all the way up to the little room at the top. The giant golden bell fills the tower, it seems bigger than me. Looking out from the belfry, I can see for miles, far beyond Roma's ballfields and all the way up the mountain road to my neighborhood on Miller's End.

Giving it a push with my Mickey Mantle, I barely move the massive bell. I try again, this time down lower, and the bell starts to sway just a little. With each push, the back-and-forth motion grows stronger. On my eighth push, I hear my first clang, actually more of a dong than a clang but at least it made a noise. I give it three more mighty Mickey Mantle swings and turn to get back down the stairs before somebody comes up and catches me. Just as I take my first step away, the bell comes back and hits my Mickey Mantle out of my hands, dropping my bat down the dark shaft beneath the swinging golden bell, now tolling loudly, already on its fourth dong. I can't even see my Mickey Mantle bat down the dark shaft, and the massive bell nearly hits me in the head every time I try to look.

I can hear Sonny telling me, "It doesn't count if you get caught, Sammy." It's time to go. I run down the stairs and out of Town Hall just as the golden bell hits its tenth dong. Mission accomplished. My game-winning home run streak of one is now a legend. It's time to get home for the big game.

The golden bell is still donging as I ride my bike fast down Main Street peddling as far away from Town Hall as I can get. That's gotta be twenty dongs already. I'm gonna hit lots more game winners now.

I stop at the corner of Mountain Road and look back at Town Hall. Two boys in Babylon Wasp uniforms are going in the side door where I just left. I recognize them, it's Conrad and Satchmo, the big-mouthed catcher and his laughing pitcher. They probably think I'm still up there ringing the bell, and they want to mess with me. Stupid kids, they're definitely gonna get caught. It's time to go. I peddle straight up the mountain road and make it home in record time to watch the Braves game. Strange though, the bell is still donging when I get home. Why is it still ringing? Did my Mickey Mantle bat cause that much motion? I better go back and try to get it out when the game is over.

It's already the fourth inning by the time I get home

and tell my mom all about my grand slam. We do our home run dance in the kitchen, the same one she always used to do with Sonny. Mom sets me up in front of the T.V with my Mac 'N Cheese just as he steps up to the plate for his second at bat of the game. Lucky for me he hasn't hit it already. The Dodgers have Al Downing pitching, he throws mostly fastballs. Hammerin Hank loves those fastballs, most of his homers have come off the fastball. He takes the first pitch, deciding not to swing. It's a strike, right down the middle of the plate. That would have been a juicy one to hit but Hank wants to see Downing's fastball before he takes his big swing. He knows just how big this moment is. Hank then steps out of the batter's box, takes a few deep breaths, squares his shoulders, steps back in, sets his feet and gets his bat ready, exactly the same way I do. Downing locks eyes with Hank for what seems like a full minute, then goes into his windup and throws what looks like another fastball. Whap...Hammerin Hank meets it with a thunderous swat, crushing the ball off his bat on a line drive heading toward the left centerfield wall. Maybe, just maybe, this is it. Bill Buckner, the Dodgers left fielder, runs back to the wall and jumps up. Did he get it? No, not even close. It's over the wall into the bullpen. Hammerin Hank Aaron has just hit his 715th home run, breaking Babe Ruth's record and I got to see it happen. Even better, he did it on an 0-1 strike count just like me, only mine was a walk-off grand slam to win the game. Just saying. But tonight, Hank Aaron is the new major league home run champion, and he's black just like me. Mom and I do our home run dance again, this time for Hammerin Hank Aaron.

We watch him round the bases in his signature trot, faster than some guys run to first base. Hank was always fast.

A few fans climb out of the stands to run with him. Fans in Atlanta and all across the country are going wild. Henry 'Hank' Aaron just broke Babe Ruth's home run record, the one that nobody thought could ever be broken, the one that lasted for 39 years since 1935. Hank did it, and he did it on my best day ever. I feel like me and Hank Aaron are one in the same…and I can hear the big golden bell still ringing. Is it ringing for Hammerin Hank now? I better go get my Mickey Mantle bat out of there, or it might never stop ringing.

The fourth inning ends with the Braves taking the lead over the Dodgers on Hank's record breaking home run smash. If I'm quick and nobody's there, I can climb the belfry stairway one more time, scoop up my Mickey Mantle bat, and then the bell should stop clanging. But somebody must have noticed by now. If I see any cars or people anywhere near Town Hall, I'll just peddle by like I'm out for my evening bike ride, having nothing to do with that bell still ringing.

My bicycle glides down the mountain road in the humid April night air as the last gasp of dusk gives away to darkness. I take my hands off the handlebars and spread my arms out wide like I'm flying far above Roma, all the way to Atlanta to congratulate Hank on his home run. As I come into town, I notice Main Street is blocked off to traffic and I immediately see why—the belfry is on fire. All three of our fire engines plus another two from Babylon are parked in front of Town Hall spraying their water guns up at the belfry, which is completely covered in flames. It's the water pressure from the powerful truck hoses that is pushing the golden bell back and forth as the firemen try to douse the flames, which are burning high into the night sky.

I push my bike down Main Street to move closer. Did I

cause all of this by dropping my Mickey Mantle bat down the shaft? Did anyone see me? I remember seeing those Wasps, Satchmo and Conrad, climbing the belfry staircase after I already came out.

A voice from behind me asks, "Did you see Hank's homer?"

I turn to see Jimmy Blake who scored on my grand slam. Like me, he's still wearing his uniform.

"I just watched it at home. What a beaut; Buckner never had a chance of catching it. Why did he even jump? What happened here, Jimmy?"

"Oh, someone's in big trouble. Some kids were smoking up there in the belfry and they dropped matches and cigarettes down the shaft. It caught fire from all the paper and other stuff that's fallen down there over the years. I heard Chief Gallo telling the mayor about it."

"I wasn't smoking, I never smoke."

"I know you weren't, Sammy, I don't smoke either. I'm talking about them, over there. Those two assholes from the Wasp team we just beat. See them over there by the police car. Chief Gallo's hollering at them now. That's their pack of cigarettes he's holding. They were smoking up there in our Town Hall belfry, and they're not even from Roma. They're in big trouble now. That ought to shut Conrad up for a little while. Look, he's balling."

I look over and see the two young arsonists being led away by our police chief. Conrad is crying and loudly blaming Satchmo for dropping his lit cigarette down the shaft on purpose. Satchmo, the laughing Wasp pitcher, walks by silently, never taking his eyes off me as they get into the back of Chief Gallo's police car. Our historic wooden belfry kindled by my Mickey Mantle bat continues to blaze high up into the sky, lighting up the April night like a giant bonfire celebrating Hank Aaron's 715th home run.

Riding my bike slowly back home up the mountain road, all I can think is, I'm gonna need a new bat for the rest of the season. First thing tomorrow, I'm going to stop by Reardon's General Store to see if they have any Hank Aaron bats. If they don't, I'll order one. Me and Hank, we're gonna hit a bunch more home runs together.

I get home just in time to catch the end of the game. Hank's Braves beat the first place Dodgers 7-4, same score as we won by on my grand slam. That's one more thing me and Hammerin Hank Aaron have in common...just saying.

—APRIL 8TH 1974—
BRAVES BROADCASTER MILO HAMILTON CAPTURES THE MOMENT LIVE FROM ATLANTA-FULTON COUNTY STADIUM IN FRONT OF A SELLOUT CROWD OF 53,775 FANS PLUS NATIONAL TELEVISION AND RADIO AUDIENCES...

"He's sitting on 714. Here's the pitch by Downing. Swinging. Here's a drive to left centerfield. That ball is gonna be...outta here. It's gone. It's 715. There's a new home run champion of all time, and it's Hank Aaron...

Hammerin Hank Aaron would hit 40 more home runs over the rest of his career giving him 755 home runs, 2,297 RBI's, and 6856 total bases...all major league records.

ROMA BUDD

You've probably seen me on one of my long walks, I'm that guy in the pith helmet. If you're driving anywhere in Roma you tend to notice someone strolling up or down our mountain road. I walk everywhere. I walk because it makes me feel alive, like I'm a part of the world. I walk to spot the birds, as I am an avid birder. I also walk because I don't own a car, never even learned how to drive, and never will.

My name is Thaddius Turcott, my friends call me Tad. I've lived in Roma all my life, an original Romite and damn proud of it. I was born and raised here, a true townie. The way I see it, it's all about living in a beautiful place. The rest of it—money, power, sex, and so on—none of it matters if you're surrounded by ugliness, which most cities and all suburbs are…ugly, that is. Give me a mountaintop and a view that goes on forever and I'm a happy camper. The only problem with growing up in a town like Roma is you never want to leave it. I'm okay with that.

"Morning, Tad, beautiful day isn't it. You hiking all the way up today?" That's Rhonda Richter, my favorite neighbor here in our little Miller's End compound. She's wearing cutoff jeans, a bikini top and her cowgirl hat today. Rhonda takes gardening attire to a higher level.

"Maybe later I will…I'm gonna take a hike through the woods to the notch first. Someone sighted a Peregrine falcon flying over the notch yesterday. I want to see if I can spot him, or her. You don't see them this far north very often. The Peregrine falcon is the world's fastest bird, Rhonda, it can dive over two hundred miles an hour."

"I did not know that, Tad."

There's a lot to like about Rhonda and I don't mean just physically. She's one of those mother-earth types with curves in all the right places and a care-free attitude about life. My favorite part about Rhonda is when the sun's out, like it is today, she's drinking Margaritas for breakfast. I always make a point to stroll by when Rhonda's out gardening to start my day off right. I just stand there watching Rhonda Richter work the earth, digging her fingers deep beneath the moist dirt, guiding the bulbs into position, stroking, caressing...nobody gardens like Rhonda.

"Tad, oh Tad...planet Earth to Tad. I said, would you like a frosty Margarita before you set off on your trek. Gonna be a hot one today, somewhere in the nineties. Jeez, Tad, you really do get out there, don't you."

She motions me over to the porch where a blender holds her morning glory.

"Here, sip on this and stop fantasizing about me. I'm right here."

"I'm sorry, Rhonda, I was lost in your gardening skills for a moment there. Nobody tills the soil quite like you do. Best neighbor ever. Yeah, it's gonna be a hot one today. You working?" Rhonda's a bartender at Grady's Pub in town. She's the reason Grady's Happy Hour is so busy.

"Nah, Tuesday's my day off. I told you that last week Tad, and the week before that. You're not a real good listener, are you, Tad? Oh sure you look like you're listening but your mind's always somewhere else."

"What? I'm kidding, I heard every word you said. I just forgot today was Tuesday." I light up a doob and blow the smoke into my Margi, inhaling fumes off the frosted tequila in my glass.

"Now that's the way to start the day. I swear, Rhonda, you make me want to take up gardening. I am thinking of fixing up the yard. Maybe you could help me. You do look really good covered in dirt."

Normally I'd hangout with Rhonda longer, sometimes even the whole morning. But today I have a little private gardening of my own to do. We drink another Margarita for good luck and finish off the joint. I almost herniate myself carrying over a bag of mulch for Rhonda, and then I'm off. There's business to take care of today.

On the road again…there's something about walking that makes you notice things more than when you're in a car. There's bunny rabbits, deer, maybe a moose or two, and always the birds, lots of chirping birds. Is that a woodpecker I hear as I pass by Mr. Miller's house? Old Man Miller's sitting on his front porch, just like always. He's our very own neighborhood watch.

"Morning, Mr. Miller. Beautiful day."

"A little too hot for me, Tad. A hundred years ago it never got this hot in August, in Vermont. Where are you off to so early, Tad, and why are you all dressed up like that?"

"This is my bird watching outfit, Mr. Miller, you know that. I'm heading up to the Notch. Somebody saw a Peregrine and I want to confirm it. Hope he's still up there. Falcons move around a lot. We hardly ever get to see them around Roma. Hear that? It's a woodpecker, a Red-belly I think. You can tell by the number of pecks each time. Count them; more than six that's a Red-belly. Gotta go now, Mr. Miller, you take her easy today."

"You sure do like the birds, Tad, and Rhonda too. Don't spend too much time in the woods, storm's coming in by dinnertime. Gonna be a doozy."

In all the years I've known him, Mr. Miller's never once been wrong about the weather, unlike those clowns on TV. Just as I start my walk up the mountain road, somebody honks at me from behind.

"Yo, Tad, you're killing me with that outfit. Must be birdwatching day."

I turn around to see Frankie Gallo, my mailman, another Miller's End neighbor, driving his jeep with the steering wheel on the wrong side so he can reach the mailboxes. Those mail jeeps are sneaky quiet, you can't hear them until they're right up on top of you.

"What's up, Frankie? You gotta stop sneaking up on people like that. I told you already, I wear the knee-high socks so I don't cut up my legs walking through the bush. The pith helmet makes sure I don't get sunburned, and the blaze-orange vest is so nobody shoots me, or in your case, runs me over. The Bermuda shorts are just because it's so sticky hot today. By the way, aren't you driving on the wrong side of the road?"

"I'm the mailman, damn it. I can drive anywhere I want. The mail must go through and all that. You look like a lunatic dressed like that, Tad. Don't scare all the birds away from Roma."

"The birds don't see me coming, Frankie, that's the point. I'm watching them and they don't know it. Oh darn, here comes a car, maybe you should get out of their lane. Did I get any mail today?"

"Did you get any mail? Everybody gets mail whether they like it or not. If I remember right, you got a phone bill, your

48

bank statement, and a letter from Canada, Vancouver, I think. Shoot, I have to go. Please come up with a new look, Tad, for the good of Roma."

Frankie hits the gas and jumps back into his lane just as the oncoming car driven by Henry Huntington passes by. The Huntingtons own a huge mansion on top of the mountain road. Henry, their son, drives like a maniac all over town, so it's poetic justice Frankie gives him a taste of his own medicine. They honk at each other and exchange middle fingers, then go their separate ways. Peace and quiet are restored to my walk. I can hear my woodpecker hard at work once again. He's much closer now. That's definitely a Red-belly.

A letter from Vancouver, I know who that is, it's my buddy Dean. We go way back. Dean used to live in Roma. His letters are always the best. Dean's not much of a writer but he's damn good at figuring how to send that Vancouver weed through the mail without getting caught. He never uses the same address twice but if it's mailed from Vancouver I'm sure it's from Dean; probably those female seeds I asked him to send from his latest crop. Dean's quite the grower out on Vancouver Island. He must have over ten acres planted in full season, and he always hires plenty of cute girls to help him harvest. Dean's my hero, he's living the life. I can't wait to get back home and sample his letter.

I'm just hitting the woods now, dripping with sweat after my three-mile jaunt to reach the cool, tranquil forest. I love it in here getting lost in all these towering fir trees. Maybe I'll see the occasional hiker or a couple of drunk hunters, but for the most part folks around Roma steer clear of the woods because of all the hype about ticks spreading the dreaded Lyme disease. I hit the south slope's upper trail and cut deeper into the woods right behind the ski resort. About a half mile in I hit patch number one, the first one I ever planted.

The main thing you have to understand about growing Budd, especially if you're going to do it outside, is that it's a lot like having a still, one of those hillbilly moonshine stills. You have to locate your operation in a place where nobody else will ever go, so far off the beaten path there would be no reason for anybody to ever pass by, even by accident. I've got my four patches perfectly positioned on the sunny south slope of the state park land bordering Roma's ski resort. Each patch is set deep into the woods surrounded by thicket, stickers and poison ivy. A person would have to be completely lost or just plain crazy to stumble onto one of my little cannabis plantations. I'm no big-timer like Dean. He works a much larger crop and makes a hell of a lot more money than I do, but he also involves many more people. Me, I work alone. Everything's easier, faster and a whole lot safer when you work solo. Plus, you don't have to pay all those extra people.

My patches are never more than twenty by fifty feet, about the size of a modest in-ground swimming pool. By keeping things small and not overextending my horticultural footprint, I can grow a high-quality crop and service my loyal clientele. Not to brag, but I'd match my Roma Budd against that Alaska Gold or Dean's Vancouver Island Buzz any time.

I'll usually harvest just a little bit on each visit, three times a week. I wear a long backpack to carry my lunch, my water, my binoculars and a roll of plastic garbage bags. First thing I do when I arrive here is to eat my lunch because I really do work up a hunger making the long hike up the mountain. That frees up some more backpack space to stow the five pounds of Budd I'm going to harvest from my crops. I place the stalks in a double garbage bag and seal it tight to cut down on the stench. It usually takes me about an hour and a half to harvest, water, trim and pack up; then, I'm on the trail again headed to my next plot located three kilometers away, just over the ridge. As I start my hike, I wonder what Rhonda is doing right now.

The key to covering a lot of ground in a short amount of time is your footwear; you've got to have comfortable waterproof boots. I go with the Hightop Timberland Hiker which comes with that lifetime guarantee. I'm on my second pair in ten years and I'm pretty tough on them. I walk across the wetlands, through the mud, over the rocks, into the streams and my Timberlands just keep on trekking.

Frankie Gallo and everyone else can go right ahead and make fun of my outfit, but if you were to see me walking up and down Mountain Road on a regular basis three times a week, you'd think birdwatcher right away. I dangle the binoculars around my neck to complete the image. Roma folks have gotten used to seeing me on my treks and say, "Oh there's Tad on another one of his birdwatching adventures." I figured out a long time ago that you can do anything you want in life so long as people can pigeonhole you, make sense of what you're doing without giving it a second thought. The more harmless you look, the better off you are for being left alone, and there's no one less harmless than a birdwatcher. Is that a Boreal chickadee I hear belting out his mating call? Why, I believe it is.

August has been good for my crops so far, not too much rain and the days have been long and sunny. Everyone in Roma was ready for all this sunshine after the horrendous winter we had with one major blizzard after another. Even Old

Man Miller said he'd never seen anything like it, though he did recollect the Great Blizzard of 1863 lasted for ten days and killed all the farm animals. I think Mr. Miller's memory takes him to places he's never been. I did look it up though, there was a ten-day blizzard that hit Roma in 1863. Old Man Miller, he knows his history.

As I come out of the woods, I hear the fire alarm sound from the station down in town. I wonder whose house is on fire today. Lately, it seems like whenever someone gets into a cash crunch in Roma, their house mysteriously, or usually electrically, goes up in smoke. They announce great plans to rebuild their beloved home, but soon as they collect that fat insurance check they pack off to Florida. Why anyone would leave Roma for Florida I just can't figure out. A siren goes off behind me. It's not a fire engine siren; it's the beeping siren of a police car and he's flashing his blue lights–at me!

"Thaddius Turcott, you been starting fires again?" I turn slowly to see Chief Gallo, Frankie's Dad, our very own Andy of Mayberry, leaning his head out of the patrol car. There's another fire up at the resort. Get in, I'll give you a ride."

I tug the straps on my backpack, pulling it tight to my shoulders and take in a deep breath. The marijuana aroma from my freshly trimmed Budd envelops me like the cloud that hovers over Pigpen in those Charlie Brown cartoons. I have my backpack lined with neoprene from some old wetsuits as a protective layer but you can still smell the weed, even through the double-sealed garbage bags. There's no way I can get in Chief Gallo's police car without stinking it up .

"Nah, I don't even own a lighter, Chief. Maybe one of those city folk lit up their couch or rewired their toaster again. Is it a big fire?"

Chief Gallo goes comatose for a few seconds as he listens to the radio chatter. I stand frozen in place, taking in deep breaths trying to consume the fumes before they drift over to the Chief.

"Sounds like two condos on fire. I've got to get up there and do some crowd control. You want a ride up or not, Tad?"

"No thanks...today's my birdwatching day, Chief. Can't spot them from the car. I hear there's a Peregrine falcon buzzing around. Saw two Boreal owls last week. They come out at dusk..."

"Gotta go, Tad. Good luck with your birds." Chief Gallo flips on his siren again, guns his motor and he's off in a blue flash, speeding his way up the mountain road to the resort. As cops go, you have got to like our Chief Gallo. He's always friendly to locals, and he lives just two houses down from me on Miller's End with his big family. Sometimes I'll even point out a rare bird, or show him photos I snapped on one of my hikes of a Bicknell thrush or the elusive Gray jay.

I'm back in the woods now, heading up the Long Trail to my second patch. I'm gonna retire this one soon. They're building all these condos for the new gated community up here near the resort, and the woods nearby are disappearing fast. Now you have all these young families with kids moving into their new Roma homes, and those kids just love to explore deep into the woods. That's a big problem for me because kids don't care what they have to crawl through or climb over to get to where they're not supposed to be. It's those middle-school kids, that nine to fourteen age group that worry me the most. If they ever found one of my patches they'd know exactly the treasure it was and what to do with it. I do not need that kind of a problem. Their young and still-developing minds aren't ready for what I grow. My clientele is a bit more advanced in age, say mid-thirties to early sixties. Their minds are all done forming.

For the life of me, I cannot understand why the government doesn't legalize marijuana; then at least they could control and profit from it instead of messing up people's lives with laws that make no sense. Hell, they've legalized everything else. Marijuana is the perfect cash crop. All you have to do is control your distribution and deliver quality product. Over the years, I've built up a family of fifty or so customers. I know them all well, they know and trust me. I'd say they're all very satisfied with the service I provide. Why wouldn't they be? They buy directly from me, the grower, they pay a fair price, in cash, and I deliver. Hell, I even roll joints for some of them because they never learned how. Now that's full service, farm to table at its best, capitalism in its purest niche marketing form. I do believe Adam Smith would be proud of my business model; so why would the government make it and keep it illegal? Makes no sense to me.

It's getting on toward four o'clock now, I better work fast. I see some dark thunder clouds rolling over the mountains. As usual Old Man Miller was right, though the storm's arriving a bit earlier than he forecast.

I do a quick check to make sure the rain barrels are positioned right, and check that the siphon hose running to my plants is clear. You can't grow anything without water, and rainwater is the absolute purest; it's why my Roma Budd is like no other. I stash my tools in the tree trunk I hollowed out. I keep a separate set of tools at each plot because, in general, you don't see birdwatchers carrying garden tools. There's no time left to make my other two patches today, I have to beat this storm home. I take a few seconds to finish off a joint and enjoy the scenery. I'm going to miss this spot when I close her down, she has the best view of all four patches. I look up to check the storm clouds and spot a gaggle of Canadian snow geese flying south. It's a bit early for their winter migration. Maybe they know something about winter coming early that we don't, not even Mr. Miller. The clouds are darker now and moving in faster. I'd better get going. I have miles to go before I'm home and I'm carrying almost eight pounds of Budd, more than I planned on.

As I come out of the woods onto the mountain road, I feel the first raindrops and hear the thunder claps overhead. Shit, I've still got about two miles to make before I'm home. This isn't good. I'm gonna have to tough it out and walk faster than usual or the downpour is going to soak me. It's eerily quiet now; all the birds have already taken to shelter except for one lone Bicknell thrush watching me from his perch on a giant elm as I jog on by. Leave it to the Bicknell to be the last bird standing with his gaudy-colored plumage, just daring the storm to rain on him. A car behind me honks and I think it's Chief Gallo again. I'm fucked, this time he won't take no for an answer.

"Tad, oh Tad–earth to Tad. I bet you want a ride right about now." I'm not wondering what Rhonda's doing anymore. I can see her, and she's never looked better driving her Jeep, offering me a ride. She's like a dream come true, and she's even got a pizza, I can smell it. I throw my pack in her back seat and jump up front with Rhonda just as the rain lets loose and lightning flashes above the mountains. This is a good time not to be in the woods with that lightning doing its work.

"Damn, you have good timing, Rhonda. I was about to take shelter with the critters and wait this storm out. This is way better. It's been a long day." I spark a joint and pass it over to Rhonda.

"How about you come over to my place for dinner tonight, Tad, and I'll see if we can un-herniate your groin. How's that feeling anyway?"

"You know what, Rhonda? I completely forgot about it, but now that you mention it, I do believe some of that therapeutic massage you've been studying might just help. How about you drop me off, I'll get cleaned up and I'll be over in a half hour. That pizza sure smells good."

We turn onto Miller's End and wave to Old Man Miller as we drive by. He's sitting on his front porch just like always but tonight he's got music playing, pretty loud too. It's Elvis, what's that song, "Suspicious Minds." I always liked that one. Mr. Miller's rocking to Elvis, go figure.

"Hey Tad, don't forget your pack. It smells pretty good."

I guess maybe Rhonda's figured out what I really do on my birdwatching hikes. I grab my backpack and race inside as the rain pours down. Home at last. I see the mail Frankie Gallo delivered on my front porch and spot the letter from Dean in the insulated brown envelope. I sniff the letter and smell nothing. Deano is a master of suffocating the odor. I'm excited to see how many seeds he sent me. I'll plant them next week in the new patch I'm setting up. As I read Dean's letter, I can't believe the words, but then again, I did warn him more than a few times...

Dear Tad: How's my ski buddy? I guess you were right, smaller is better. Three of my pickers got popped last week, all of them former girlfriends, and it took about twenty minutes for them to give me up as the Big Kahuna. Even with B.C.'s lax marijuana laws, it looks like I'm going to be incarcerated up here for about two years, maybe three depending on which prosecutor I get. I'm sending you this letter through my lawyer. She's a pretty good one, so don't worry. You're my Vermont ski buddy who enjoys a good toke every once in a while, that's all. No law against that, up here anyway. Take care of yourself, Tad. I'll stay in touch and those Canadian females we talked about should be arriving next week, along with the address where you can write me. Hold on to it, I'll be there a while...then I'll come visit you.

In Carceration, Your Vancouver Budd, Dean

P.S. When I get out, I'm gonna become a birdwatcher just like my *Roma Budd. See Ya Tad.*

In the background I hear David Brinkley reporting on NBC's evening news...

—Elvis Presley died today, August 16th, 1977, his doctor announced at 3PM this afternoon. He apparently died of a heart attack. Mr. Presley was found at Graceland, his home in Memphis not breathing. His road manager tried to revive him and failed. The hospital then tried to revive him, they failed. Elvis Presley, was 42 years old and leaves behind one daughter, Lisa Marie Presley.

I walk outside and collapse onto my front porch couch. For some reason the death of Elvis hits me harder than the news of Dean going to jail. I knew Deano's days were numbered; he was always so visible in what he was doing, and involved too many people. But Elvis, I thought he'd live forever. Instead, he's dead at forty-two. The rain has stopped now, and there's a brilliant rainbow sprawled atop our mountain notch. I grab my binoculars to study the colors closely. Just a few hundred yards away, a large majestic bird soars into view. Is that the Peregrine everyone has been spotting? It must be. But wait, the colors are all wrong, and he's flying much higher than Peregrine do. My God, that's a Golden eagle, hardly ever seen in Vermont. He's a big strong one, beautiful too. He flaps his broad wings six or seven times, then soars across the towering rainbow into the blood-orange sunset. I hear Old Man Miller's music playing even louder, serenading our whole neighborhood, and now I understand why. It is in tribute to Elvis, whose pure soulful voice sings the hymn-like "If I Can Dream," as I witness that rare Golden eagle spread his powerful wings to climb higher and higher, reaching the mountaintop, then disappearing into the rainbow's regal golden arc. I wipe back a tear and whisper to no one, "Thank you Elvis. Thank you very much...for everything."

LAST STOP ROMA

"Tickets please, all tickets."

I watch the lights of Montreal shine bright and brilliant as we cross the frozen St. Lawrence River heading south to the border. A light snow falls and a steady wind blows across the glistening track, setting the wintry scene for tonight's final journey aboard the Green Mountain Local.

I've been the head conductor, actually the only conductor, on this train for thirty years now—from the first day of operation to this last run we're making tonight. They call us "The Milkrun" because we stop at so many small Vermont towns. We're the kinder, gentler version of the popular Adirondack Express which tracks on the other side of Lake Champlain, then along the Hudson all the way down to New York City. That's a ten hour trip, one way. My Green Mountain Local takes just three hours to travel from Montreal to Roma, making ten stops in between.

The city lights of Montreal fade into the distance as I begin my final march from the caboose to our lead car, punching tickets and calling out next stops to passengers I will never see again.

"All tickets please...first stop is the St. Albans border crossing. Please have your passports ready."

"How long will it be until we reach the border, Sir?"

"Plenty of time Ma'am, about an hour. We won't reach St. Albans until ten o'clock. Usually it takes about thirty minutes to clear the border and then we're on our way. Let's see, your ticket says you're headed to Burlington tonight. We should be arriving in Burlington at 11:05. Enjoy your journey and welcome aboard the Green Mountain Local."

I stop between cars to stargaze out over the prairie land stretching for miles on both sides of the track. With the storm's shimmering ice laying a topcoat over frozen farmland, the empty fields conjure a skating rink that goes on forever into the starry night. Strange how these vast tracts of prairie farmland can be located so close to a large, bustling city like Montreal. That would never happen in the U.S. where the land is either suburban sprawl or completely undeveloped outside the major cities, never actual working farmland. Over my years of traveling between Canada and the U.S., I've come to understand that not only are we very different countries in many ways, but truly separate worlds, perhaps even distant planets.

"Well hello, Freddy Falcone. Haven't seen you in a while. What brings you aboard the MilkRunner tonight, Freddie?"

"Are you kidding me, Otis? I wouldn't have missed it for the world. It's my last chance to travel back to Roma before they retire our Green Mountain Local. I'm gonna miss her, Otis, gonna miss you too. Every time I needed to get back home to see family and remember the good times, this train got me there. Have one with me Otis...I mixed up a special batch for the journey. I call it the NightTrain Whistle, because it makes you feel like whistling as it's going down."

"Nah, I better not, Freddy. There's no drinking allowed on duty and all that. Technically, I am still on duty until we pull into Roma at midnight...Oh, what the hell, one's not going to hurt, might even help. Make mine a double, out of respect for the MilkRunner's swan song. To hell with the rules tonight. If I'm going to break them, might as well break them in half."

"That's the attitude, Otis...I always liked you. I still can't believe they're closing this line down. There's no other train like it running through small-town Vermont all the way up to Montreal. How are we supposed to get back home now? I will not travel by bus, I hate those buses."

"I know Freddy, me too. I don't know anyone who likes buses. But they're cheaper to run and that's all they care about anymore. This is pretty good, Freddy; tastes like a Black Russian with more of a kick to it."

"That's the NightTrain Whistle, choo-choo. It's the potato vodka that gives it that extra kick. You gotta go with the potato vodka, Otis."

"I gotta go punch some more tickets before we reach the border, Freddy. Thanks for the drink, I mean the NightTrain Whistle. Choo-choo."

Freddy's been riding this train almost as long as I have. He's always in that same window seat too, fourth car in the back, away from everyone. I don't even check his ticket anymore. Freddy is royalty on this train, like the rest of my Roma regulars. He taught something mathematical, not sure exactly what, at McGill University up there in Montreal. Once a month, Freddy likes to get back to Roma where he grew up and his family still lives. By the time we reach the end of the line, there's only Freddy and a handful of others still on the train with me.

It's funny how everybody gets so nervous at our border crossing in St. Albans, even when they don't have anything to hide. Not Freddy and my Roma passengers though. They don't care about borders or anything else when they're riding this train. They just want to get back home to Roma.

I know all of the Customs guys at our border crossing.

They're a good bunch, always ready to crack a joke, but you'd never know it when they board our train and ask for passports and reason for travel. Suddenly they become stern and make passengers forget where they are going and why they're going there, petrified that their papers are not in order. The Customs guys enjoy this little charade they get to play, knowing most of our passengers are Canadians and Vermonters, local folk. The only crime they might be committing on any given crossing is smuggling pure maple syrup or smoked-meat poutine.

They go through the train fast. I say goodnight to them one last time, then it's hand shakes all around to honor the end of our working together. That only took twenty minutes, a new record for the Green Mountain Local, one that is sure to stand.

Strange to think how tonight, at midnight, it all comes to a screeching halt. This train has been my life, four days a week—Sunday, Monday, Thursday and Friday; two round trips a day running from Roma to Montreal, each trip taking three hours one way, six hours round trip to make for a twelve-hour day. I would always sleep in the caboose on my days off instead of hiking up the Mountain Road to my parent's place on Miller's End. They're both gone now. They left the house to me, the home I grew up in. But without them, it feels so empty. The caboose feels more like home to me now. It's cozy. There's nothing quieter or darker than a deserted train station at midnight when all the people have departed and the trains have stopped running. Once that last passenger exits the train and I say goodnight to Wendell, my engineer, I bed down for the night on the bunk bed in the caboose and let the silence take me away into a deep sleep.

"Tickets, all tickets please. Next stop-Colchester."

"Hello, Otis. I need to buy a ticket tonight. I just never

seem to be on time to make the ticket window in the station."

"Well hello, Mrs. Purdy. Looks like you've been shopping up there in Montreal. Is that a new hat?"

"Why yes it is, Otis, thank you for noticing. I just bought a few things for the grandchildren. The holidays are here before you know it. Time goes by so quickly; suddenly the kids are all grown up and they have no time for grandma anymore. I like to surprise them with some gifts under the tree so they know I'm always with them."

"I think it was this same time last year when you were heading home for the holidays, Mrs. Purdy. We're running ahead of schedule tonight, so just sit back and enjoy the ride, our last one."

"I know, Otis, I heard it in the wind as they say. Don't worry though, you'll be alright and we will be too. You've always taken such good care of us, your Roma travelers, so it's only right we do the same for you, Otis."

Mrs. Purdy was a good friend of my mom and dad. She was a schoolteacher in Roma for so many years and was my fourth and fifth grade homeroom teacher. Every time I see her, always around the holidays, she's wearing a new hat suited more for the spring then these winter months. We make Colchester ten minutes ahead of schedule. Only a few passengers get off. Most of the people riding tonight's train are headed to Burlington.

"Next stop-Winooski. Platform on the right side. Watch your step."

In a strange way, you could say I've been married to this train for the last thirty years, and they've all been good ones. I came to understand a long time ago that not everyone finds that certain someone to love in their life, that special person who loves them back. I didn't, and I tried my best. So there comes a day when you accept that if you're not going to find someone, you better find something to love, some special thing that makes you feel alive, included and needed. This train and these passengers bound for Roma, traveling home to the families they love, have given me that feeling and so much more. I've found my peace on this train. After tonight, I don't have a clue what I'll do, or where I'll go next.

We pickup a few passengers in Winooski for the short hop to Burlington. They're mostly students heading back to Burlington for classes tomorrow. I punch their tickets and pause to listen to a bit of the Monday Night Football game one of the kids has tuned in on his radio. He tells me the Pats are leading the Dolphins 6-0 at halftime. If the Patriots win this game tonight they just might make the playoffs, so it's a pretty big game.

"Next stop-Burlington. Exit to platform on your left, and watch your step."

We are heading into a stronger snowfall now. I notice Wendell has slowed the train down a bit. We're still on schedule but have lost our early arrival time. The fastest trip we've ever recorded station to station from Montreal to Roma is two hours and forty-four minutes, back in May of 1975. Before Wendell put the breaks on, we were on track to break that record by a good five minutes. I guess it's better to be safe than early on our last milkrun.

"Burlington Station...all off for Burlington. Thank you for riding the Green Mountain Local and have a good night."

The four cars are almost empty now, as most of my passengers tonight were bound for Burlington, home to the University of Vermont. The queen city sits on the shores of Lake

Champlain, which is the boundary separating Vermont from the state of New York. There's talk of taking our passenger cars and adding them to the New York Adirondack Line, along with an even faster engine. But there's no such talk of transferring Wendell and me over with those cars. We are being retired tonight. The stations go by faster now, just empty platforms sitting lifeless in the silence of the night. Only a few passengers remain on board; most of them are headed for our last stop, Roma.

I spot Tucker Turcott sitting in his usual seat midway through the first car. Tucker ran the ski school up at the mountain until his car accident a few years ago. He taught me, his son, Tad, and most of the kids who grew up in Roma how to ski and follow the rules so everyone could make it down the mountain safely. Tucker's still wearing his ski-school hat and jacket, staring out the window at the sleeping towns as we travel closer to home.

"Next Stop-Charlotte."
"Next Stop-Hinesburg."
"Next Stop-Sienna Falls."
"Next Stop-Trusca."
"Next Stop-Waterbury."

Walking back to my caboose, I spot Elizabeth Engel in the third car. How could I have missed her before?

"Hello Elizabeth, it's good to see you again. I was wondering if you were going to make it back to Roma tonight. This is it you know, our farewell tour."

"Yes I know, Otis. I'm going to miss this old train. She's a friendly train, the way train service should be. You too, Otis, you've made our journeys peaceful and always so welcoming the way you guide us back to Roma for our visits. It's been an honor knowing you and traveling with you, Otis."

"Thank You, Elizabeth. I feel the same way. My Roma passengers are always my favorites. You've become my family, my whole world really; you especially."

I make it back to my caboose car at 11:30 just as we leave Waterbury Station for the climb up the mountain to Roma. My radio is tuned into the Monday Night Football game. Frank Gifford the golden boy announcer says the score is tied thirteen all, with only a few seconds remaining. New England is getting ready to kick a twenty-seven yard field goal to win the game and put them in the playoffs. Twenty-seven yards is a chip shot, I could make that. The Patriots are going to win and make the playoffs. It's a big night for New England. But just before the kick, Frank Gifford says to his co-announcer, Howard Cosell...

GIFFORD—Timeout is called with three seconds left...and I don't care what's on the line Howard, you have got to say what we both know in the booth...

COSELL—Yes, we have to say it. Remember, this is just a football game, no matter who wins or loses. An unspeakable tragedy confirmed by ABC news in New York City. John Lennon was shot twice outside of his apartment on the West Side of New York City. The most famous perhaps of all the Beatles, he was rushed to Roosevelt Hospital and pronounced Dead On Arrival, tonight, December 8th, 1980. Hard to get back to the game after that news flash which duty bound, we had to deliver. Frank?

GIFFORD—Indeed it is Howard.

I am shocked by the news; he was my favorite Beatle. It was John Lennon who wrote all the best Beatles songs..."Help", "All You Need Is Love", "Day In The Life", and "Imagine." They were all written by Lennon, though I'm pretty sure he wrote *"Imagine"* after the Beatles broke up. What idiot would shoot John Lennon, and why? All the guy ever sang about was peace and love. I need another one of Freddy's NightTrain Whistles, maybe two.

I feel the tears I've been holding back all night streaming out now. It is time to weep openly for John Lennon, for the end of the happiest time of my life, for the demise of my beloved Vermont Local. John Lennon is dead. Where will I go from here? What will I do tomorrow and the next day? It is almost midnight now. We will soon be at our last stop, Roma.

The radio stations are all playing Beatles and John Lennon songs in tribute. Turning the dial, I find a news station… John Lennon was only forty years old…he was shot by someone named Mark David Chapman, not twice as Howard Cosell said but in fact four times in the back…only a coward shoots someone in the back…John Lennon was shot in the entrance to his New York City apartment building, The Dakota, as he was coming home…John Lennon was shot at 10:40PM and pronounced dead at 11:15PM on Monday, December 8th, 1980. Howard Cosell's announcement on Monday Night Football, the very first one made, came just fifteen minutes later at 11:30PM.

I was a little too old to be a Beatles fan when they became famous in 1964, but I immediately became a John Lennon fan. He was the coolest of the Beatles, and he put out even better music after they broke up. I turn the radio dial away from the somber news coverage and land on my all-time favorite John Lennon song as we pull into Roma station ahead of schedule. It is one minute before midnight…

Imagine there's no heaven
It's easy if you try

No hell below us
Above us only sky
Imaging all the people
Living for today...

Standing on the platform outside my caboose car I watch as my Roma passengers exit the train and walk in different directions away from the station, disappearing into the winter night—Professor Freddy, Mrs. Purdy, Tucker Turcott and Elizabeth Engel—all solid citizens of Roma returning home once again to remember and relive the best moments of their lives...

Imagine there's no countries
It isn't hard to do
Nothing to kill or die for
And no religion too
Imagine all the people
Living life in peace...

Out of respect, I had read and kept each of their obituaries. These were people who defined Roma at its best. Mrs. Purdy taught hundreds of kids how to play the piano. Professor Freddy taught mathematics at every academic level from elementary to university. Tucker Turcott made skiers out of kids who could barely ride their bicycles without falling. And Elizabeth Engel, she taught me that being alone doesn't have to mean that you are lonely. She was the first to depart during our childhood days and the first of the midnight Roma passengers to appear on my train and make me feel needed to help her make the journey home...

You may say I'm a dreamer
But I'm not the only one
I hope someday you'll join us
And the world will live as one

"Imagine" is still playing on the radio as I lay my heavy head on the pillow, desperate for the deep slumber that will provide my escape from this tragic night. I will sleep here in my caboose compartment tonight, tomorrow and the next day too, until they make me leave. What do you do when the life you have known and loved suddenly comes to an end?

Imagine no possessions
I wonder if you can
No need for greed of hunger
A brotherhood of man
Imagine all the people
Sharing all the world

You move forward is what you do, hoping that things will get better, doors will open and people will welcome you home. As I close my eyes, I can see Elizabeth Engel, my childhood sweetheart, beckoning me from outside the caboose window. The snow is falling, the moon is full as we walk hand-in-hand up the mountain road to my parent's home where life began for me on Miller's End. I have found my peace...

You may say I'm a dreamer
But I'm not the only one
I hope someday you'll join us
And the world will live as one.

HAPPY HOUR AT GRADY'S

I heard about it as I was getting ready for work. It was early afternoon on a crystal-clear late January Sunday when I turned on the television and heard the news—the space shuttle Challenger had blown up just after takeoff, killing all seven people on board. They kept showing the launch of the rocket climbing higher with all systems-go, then just a minute after takeoff the Challenger exploded into pieces. I stood in front of my television set, naked and in shock, watching that same clip over and over showing what had happened that morning. All seven crew members were dead; one of them a teacher from New Hampshire. An hour later I was still frozen in place, still undressed watching the news reports and realizing I had better get moving if I was going to make it to work on time. Somehow that still mattered.

Everyone comes to Grady's for Happy Hour. Some come for our free appetizers, others for the exotic umbrella drinks, and a chosen few come to Grady's every Thursday through Sunday from 3PM to 7PM because that's when I'm working. They know they better come put tips in my jar or there just might be hell to pay.

I love my work schedule, just four days a week, four hours a day. That leaves me plenty of time to do my Yoga, my gardening, my skiing and anything else I feel like doing. With all the outdoor activities right at your doorstep in Roma—the skiing, hiking, bicycling and climbing—why would anyone want to work all the time? My understanding of this capitalist deal we are all stuck in is that you work to live, not give up your whole life just to work. Why would anyone do that willingly? I've been the Happy Hour bartender at Grady's Pub for nearly ten years now. It's the best job ever. The Gradys are a great family who treat me like one of their own. We are Roma's only hotspot, the place where everyone comes to meet, and meet up. That's what Happy Hour is all about, people getting together to share what happened that day and plan what is going to happen that night. It's those nighttime plans that always catch my attention. That's when the dark secrets come out to play.

What makes Grady's Pub & Grille so popular is that everyone feels welcome here. We're a bit of a sports bar mixed with a family-style restaurant that becomes a quiet late-night rendezvous, perfect for that romantic nightcap. Grady's is everything to everyone, according to your mood. But it's Happy Hour that brings my crowd in. My deal with Grady's is that I get to work Happy Hour all by myself and all the tips are mine. I don't even get an hourly wage. My money comes exclusively from the tip jar, which means it's all cash and completely off the books. It's one of those rare win-win-win situations. I sell many expensive exotic drinks, the Grady's make lots of money from the bar, and my regulars stuff my jar with dollars meant to buy my silence. One thing about me, I do know how to keep a secret, if you pay me. Most good bartenders do.

I turn on the TV behind the bar and there it is again, the space shuttle Challenger exploding just after takeoff. They're not saying what caused the explosion but they're sure it wasn't sabotage. How do they always know that for sure so soon after something happens?

"Hello Rhonda, and may I say you're looking especially lovely today. Horrible what happened. Heads are going to roll over this. Somebody didn't do their job."

"I don't get how it could happen so quickly, so close to home. They should have seen the problem, you'd think. Very sad...what are you having today, Judge Taylor—a Zombie, the Scorpion, or how about a Texas Two-Step, one of my very own creations."

"A Texas Two-Step it is then, Rhonda, and this is for you, just because..."

Judge Taylor puts two one-hundred dollar bills in my jar and gives me a wink, the same wink he gives me every Sunday when he comes to Grady's to pay his dues. The judge isn't a bad guy, none of my regulars really are. Judge Taylor just made the mistake of playing night court with an underage waitress who loves to talk about her exploits. A few hundred dollars a week to keep me quiet and keep his after-hours court in session is nothing to the judge. Also, I think he likes being blackmailed by a large-breasted woman who makes him drink expensive umbrella cocktails on Sundays. It arouses his animal spirits. I bring my Texas Two-Step over to his table and wink back at him as he discusses ethics and morals with a group of young lawyers eager to get in the judge's good graces and perhaps someday become just like him.

Sitting over by the front window at her usual table is Stacey Sharman, our long-serving state senator. Stacey's been in office for what seems like forever. She runs on the promise of making sure the real people of Roma, and all the other small towns, are heard and represented; 'real people' means native Vermonters. Problem is, Stacey's been taking kickbacks from the large oil, gas and electric corporations to hold back development of the much smaller solar and wind-power companies. Stacey's other problem politically, is that she prefers women to men. I mean, who doesn't? But Senator Stacey has a husband and two kids at home. Her decidedly Christian-right voter base would have a fundamental problem with Stacey's little secret if they ever found out the truth. Corruption, they can forgive. What politician doesn't take a bribe here and a kickback there? That's why they become politicians in the first place, instead of getting a real job. But Senator Stacey Sharman as a lesbian, that is totally unacceptable and would bring an immediate end to her political career. It's funny how folks can forgive greed but never sexuality.

I found out firsthand about Senator Stacey's secret side. She'd had a few two many martinis at Happy Hour last year just before Christmas. That's the problem with martinis, you just can't stop drinking them, especially mine. Then you go and say too much, as the laughter suddenly stops.

It was out in the parking lot of all places where Senator Stacey came on to me. I'd served her eight martinis so I knew she was in no condition to drive, much less proposition me. Stacey started talking about all the Roma housewives she had slept with, a fairly impressive list I had to admit. I couldn't figure out how she had any time left over to attend the Senate and cast her vote with her days so filled with sexual interludes. That night I gave Senator Stacey a ride home and made it clear how surprised and upset I was about what had happened and everything she had told me. I wasn't really, but it's perception that matters most. The very next day, Senator Stacey shows up at Happy Hour full of apologies and regrets, puts her first hundred in my jar and orders our most expensive drink, the Scorpion. She's been one of my regulars ever since. Senator Stacey Sherman, voice of the people, always a hundy and always the Scorpion.

"How are you today, Senator?"

"So sad about what happened, Rhonda. All flags will be flying at half mast this week in honor of those brave astronauts and crew. It's such a tragedy. I still can't understand how something like this can happen with all those smart people working at NASA. Watch, they're going to shut down the space program now. They've been looking for a reason because it's costing too much money. Ah yes, my Scorpion, and this is for you, Rhonda."

"Thank you, Senator. I heard about it just before I came to work. I'm still in shock, I feel like I'm not completely here. Just wave when you want another. Oh, Judge Taylor over there says to say hello." The Senator looks over at the Judge. They raise their umbrella drinks and toast each other with empty smiles.

Like any relationship, clear communication is so important when you want people to understand how you feel about what they are doing. Everyone has secrets, things going on in their lives they don't want other people to know about. I never truly blackmail anyone, I don't have to. They are always ready to do it to themselves. It's the truth coming out that they fear the most. Paying me a few hundred dollars a week to keep that truth hidden seems like a good deal to them. All I ever really have to do is encourage them to take responsibility for their actions, tell the truth to their wife, husband, congregation, company, the police…it's always the sinners who come up with the payment arrangement, which I am more than happy to accept. I don't want Grady's to miss out, so I make all of my regulars drink only our most expensive exotic cocktails at Happy Hour. No craft beers for them, they must suffer the umbrella drinks. Grady's gets to keep the bar money, and I rake in my hundys, filling the tip jar. Roma has so many secrets to keep, sooner or later I'm going to hear them all. So yes, business is good.

"I'll have two Zombies, Rhonda, one for me and one for Zach."

"How's school going, Eli? Zach's studying medicine isn't he? And you're engineering?"

"You sure do have a long memory, Rhonda. Wish you didn't, but you do…Oh yeah, this is for you from me and Zach. That's twice this week."

"I'll bring your Zombies right over, Eli. Just remember, this is all part of learning from your mistakes. Why let one stupid act mess up your bright and beautiful futures. We're all here to learn from our mistakes; we're just works in progress, getting better every day.

"Thanks, Rhonda. We really do appreciate you keeping everything quiet and I promise we'll never do anything like that again. I mean never, ever."

Zach and Eli Houghton live in the new gated community up on top of the mountain road. They moved here a few years ago from Texas. The Houghton boys live off the family's oil and gas fortune that comes from an endless well of old money. Paying me four hundred dollars every week, that's just two hundred each, keeps their university lives blissful, free from media and law enforcement attention. It's a no-brainer to them. I probably should be charging more, but they're good kids and I truly do believe they've learned a valuable lesson through our little arrangement.

It was completely by accident that I caught them in their act of stupidity, the one that brought us together for

Happy Hour penance. Over the years I have found if you put two or more guys together, at any age, they will usually come up with the absolute dumbest things to do to pass the time. With brothers, that probability factor jumps even higher. They should do a scientific study to find out why that is. Women are different. We'll talk a lot, sometimes in horrible and ugly ways, but we never actually do anything so stupid as burning down the Mountain Chapel…a woman wouldn't do that.

It was just after midnight when I came out of the woods with the full moon shining a clear path on the cross-country trail. I like to ski at night all by myself with everything quiet and still. Up ahead where the nordic and alpine trails come together I could see what looked like a bonfire. It was a strange night to have one in the middle of the week, but I skied over to check it out, get warm and see if I knew anyone. As I drew closer I could see it wasn't a bonfire at all but rather a real fire, an out of control blaze burning down our Vermont landmark Mountain Chapel. There at the scene, drunk and disorderly, running into each other trying to throw snow on the flames, were Eli and Zach Houghton.

"Zach, Eli what the hell happened here? You better call the fire department now, before it's too late."

"I think it already is, Rhonda. Swear to God we didn't mean to do it. We were just messing around inside, lighting candles and smoking a joint or two when one of the candles tipped over and set the straw from the nativity scene on fire and sent sparks flying everywhere. It was an accident Rhonda. Please don't tell anyone, I promise we'll make it up to you."

"Are we running Eli?"

"Oh yeah, Zach, we're running. You better get out of here too, Rhonda."

Instead of taking off, I called the fire department from the lodge and told them the chapel was on fire. Why not? I figured I didn't have anything to hide. I was just out doing some nighttime Nordic skiing when I happened upon the fire. I never did mention seeing Eli and Zach that night. That fire happened almost two years ago, and the brothers Houghton have been paying me four hundred dollars a week ever since. The money's no problem for those boys, they spend that much and more on dinner in Burlington on any given night. We've become friends over the years, basically they're good kids. Why would I mess up their lives and reputations for one bad decision that could have been harshly judged as a hate crime instead of just a toppled candle that burned down the nativity manger?

Rhonda-justice is so much better. I keep all of their secrets buried away and serve expensive umbrella drinks to help them learn from their mistakes and misdeeds. You could say I am their judge, their jury and ultimately their penance.

"Sorry I'm late, Rhonda, had a little trouble getting out of a meeting at the bank."

"I did wonder where you were. It's Sunday, Peter, this is the only meeting that really matters. You're usually here by five. What time is it? Ten minutes to seven, you almost missed Happy Hour. How about two Long Island Iced Teas to make up for your tardiness?"

"Sounds great, Rhonda. I am really thirsty today, two Long Islands ought to do it. This is for you, of course, and I'm doubling the tip because I'm going to be out of town next week on holiday."

Peter Wellington is the Chief Investment Officer at Vermont's largest savings and loan bank. His sin is all about money and greed. Peter's gambling debts forced him to dip into the bank's pension funds and retirement accounts to the tune of millions of dollars. His hardy appetite for blackjack and roulette dug him even deeper into a money-pit, swallowing up the dollars Peter was entrusted to invest for the bank. My neighbor Monique, who works closely with Peter, even on Sundays, told me all out about it over three bottles of red wine one winter night. We talk a lot, living just across the street from each other on Miller's End. Monique says Peter is a true genius at covering up his embezzlement by always coming up with a single long- shot investment return at the end of each quarter that pays enormous profits to help him continue his financial charade. I'm pretty sure Peter and Monique are doing a whole lot more than just working after hours at the bank, but she hasn't told me anything about that, yet. Funny how people are more than willing to talk about money but want to stay oh-so private about their sex lives. Peter Wellington, he's another one of my regulars who pays dearly for his sins.

All together, I have twenty-one people in my family of Happy Hour regulars who show up at Grady's twice a week to pay their respects and put their offerings in my tip jar. It's like they're coming to church, only without the sermon. Alleluia.

With all my regulars making their weekly one-hundred and two-hundred dollar contributions, plus my normal tips, I take in almost five thousand dollars from my four day, twelve hour work week—and that's all cash. Last year that worked out to be almost two-hundred and fifty thousand dollars, all tax free since I'm not found anywhere on Grady's books as an employee. Not too bad for a girl from Roma who would rather garden and do my Yoga than work all day long. I believe everyone needs to find their place in this world and

I've found mine watching over Roma's sinners. Speaking of sinners, I did hear something last week about Reverend Digby and the leader of his church choir, who is a married man, that I found to be quite disturbing. Here comes the good Reverend now. He sure does look worried, and thirsty. Something tells me I'm going to need a bigger tip jar and a new umbrella drink. Perhaps I'll call it, the Holy Highballer...

NEWS FLASH FROM WBZ IN BOSTON—(showing video footage of explosion)
—Today, Sunday January 28th 1986, Space Shuttle Challenger exploded at 11:39AM over the Atlantic Ocean just 73 seconds after takeoff, only nine miles above Earth after its launch from Cape Canaveral in Florida. All seven crew members were killed including five NASA astronauts, one payload specialist and the first civilian schoolteacher to attempt space travel, Christa McAuliffe from New Hampshire. President Reagan has declared tomorrow a national day of mourning and promises to launch an investigation into what caused this tragic event...sabotage and foul play have already been ruled out.

DISTANT THUNDER

It's been rumbling like that for three days now. Lots of thunder but no lightning. We sure could use some rain to melt all this snow. Here we are in mid-April already and it still looks like the dead of winter out there. What ever happened to spring? Strange though, hearing all that thunder coming from the other side of the mountain but not seeing any storm, yet.

"Mr. Barrows, I'm confused by this question. When you ask what presidential proclamation freed the southern slaves in 1863 during the Civil War, are you looking for the actual name of the proclamation or the name of the president? It's very confusing, Mr. Barrows."

"I think it's pretty straightforward, Rufus. Name the proclamation. Then the next question asks you who the president was during the Civil War."

"Did we go over this in class, Mr. Barrows? I don't think we did."

"All last week and the week before that, Mr. Reardon. Think about it. It's a pretty famous proclamation and a very well-known president."

"I might have been absent those days. Maybe if you could just give me a hint."

"No, you were here, physically anyway, and I just did give you a hint. Go back to your desk, think about it and put down your honest answer. Better finish this section up, you still have to write the essay question...twenty minutes left class."

Rufus Reardon is a smart kid who always tries to squeeze some answers out of me with his probing test questions. He's gotten pretty good at it, asking one open-ended question to get a handful of helpful hints. If he'd only put as much effort into reading and actually studying for these history tests he'd be an A+ student. Just twenty minutes remain in this last period of the day, and of what was my teaching career. I received the bad news yesterday from Principal Turner who is retiring in June at the end of this school year. I'd been passed over as his replacement, the School Board had decided to go with Sally Sutherland. Sally's been teaching at Roma High School two years less than me and she's nowhere near as popular with the students. But she does what she's told no questions asked and agrees with everything the School Board says. Sally's the perfect YES-man, only she's a woman. So to hell with it all, today is the day Mr. Barrows retires from teaching. After ten memorable years at Roma High School, it clearly is time to move on. This is my last class, last test, last period before my two-thirty meeting with Principal Turner to hand in my papers, as they say. Funny how everything seems easier once you've made up your mind.

"Eyes on your own paper, Mr. Connelly."

"Trust me, Mr. Barrows, it's not Katie's test paper I was looking at."

The class lets out a laugh, everyone except Rufus Reardon, who jumps up and approaches me with yet another probing question.

"On this one, Mr. Barrows, where was the first battle of the Civil War fought and who won it? Do you mean exactly what location? Who won it, isn't that open to interpretation?"

"No it is not, Mr Reardon. There was a clear winner because one general surrendered to the other. There, I gave you something you can use in your essay. Now move forward, Rufus, the clock is ticking, for the both of us."

Odd how the thunder bursts sound a bit louder each day but the storm still keeps its distance from Roma. I wish the dark skies would open up and pour down on us to get it over with. Going to sleep and waking up in the middle of the night to the rolling sound of thunder is like waiting in the dark for a restless monster to attack. You know he's coming for you but you don't know when. At some point, you just want to deal with that moment of truth.

As I think about it, our award-winning school has been sliding down the proverbial hill steadily these past few years. We are still a cut above the rest but I have noticed our standards slipping, teachers slacking and students sliding at Roma High School. I can't put my finger on exactly what, but something has changed. The image that Roma is that shining city on the hill with the best schools in Vermont has faded.

We still say all the right things, still talk-the-talk. Our students learn about critical thinking, empathetic listening and mutual respect, but there is no real expectation that they will put it all to work in their everyday lives. That high standard of behavior posted at the school's entranceway has become tarnished and forgotten. When students, a town and an entire culture lose all hope for their lives ever getting better, they become lost and abandon those lofty guiding principles in favor of basic everyday survival.

"Five minutes left. Start finishing up your essays, everyone. You should be writing your conclusions now. No, Mr. Reardon, stay in your seat. There's no time for any more questions. Trust what you know and go with it."

Just after two o'clock the thunder clouds finally cross over the mountain top and we can see the massive storm we've been hearing these last three days. BOOM, CRASH,

BOOM...like artillery fire launched from an unseen enemy, thunder claps explode through the ominous clouds and rain pours down with a vengeance. We are in it now, the encroaching darkness surrounds us.

"I can't concentrate with all that racket outside, Mr. Barrows."

"That's alright, Chester. Time's up, pens and pencils down. Turn in your test papers on my desk. We still have ten minutes in our final period so you may speak quietly amongst yourselves. I did say quietly, Mr. Connelly."

Now comes the violent lightning, as hard rain falls in rhythm with the thunder's percussion. Usually a powerful storm like this one is fast-moving, staying only a few minutes before moving away from Roma down the mountain gap into the valley towns. But this one is different with its ferocity of rain, and even hail now. This violent storm is going to be with us for some time.

"Mr. Barrows, did you know Robert E. Lee graduated second in his class from West Point? It says so in our book, page four-hundred twenty."

BOOM, RUMBLE, CRACK...

"I'm simply thrilled that you're finally looking at our history book, Mr. Reardon. Leaf forward a few pages, why don't you. Take a look at the Civil War section and the Emancipation Proclamation signed by Abraham Lincoln in 1863."

"Damn, Emancipation Proclamation not enunciation. That's close enough though. I guessed that much because of your Honest Abe hint."

"Well done, Rufus, well done. Are all papers in?"

At two-twenty-five the classroom phone rings, a rare

occurrence, especially during 8th period. It's Principal Turner speaking in a panicky voice telling me to turn on the television news immediately. There's been a school shooting.

The thunder now sounds like it is hovering directly above our school now. Lightning penetrates through the massive black clouds that conjure attack ships firing death bolts, as solid sheets of rain flood the school's playing fields. One by one, my senior eighth-period American History students silently gather around the classroom television to witness the nightmare unfolding at Columbine High School in Littleton Colorado…

—THIS IS CNN HEADLINE NEWS ON APRIL 20TH, 1999—
Authorities in Littleton, Colorado are securing the scene at a deadly school shooting so they can make a final body count as the community and the nation struggle to come to grips with all the carnage. Authorities are searching for booby trap explosives left behind by the two suspects in the Columbine school shooting. The death toll in the shooting is now at 15 including the two teenagers who police say did the shooting. The two suspects are believed to have killed themselves. At least 24 more students were wounded by bullets or shrapnel from pipe bombs carried by the gunmen. For now, the bodies of the victims have not been removed from the school. The two gunmen were both juniors at Columbine High School. Police have identified the two students as Eric Harris and Dylan Klebold. Both were considered outcasts…

We all stand in silence as CNN interviews some of the students who escaped unharmed. It is almost two-thirty now, which means the shooting happened at Columbine High School in Colorado just a little over an hour ago factoring in the two-hour time difference. The final bell rings, jolting us all and signaling the end of our school day.

"If anyone wants to talk about this, I'll be here after my meeting with Principal Turner."

I watch my students walk away in disbelief, some in tears, some holding hands—all of them dazed and confused at what they have just witnessed. The storm rages above our award-winning school where something like this could never happen. I wonder if just yesterday Columbine High School believed that too.

Waiting outside Principal Turner's office for my requested end-of-day meeting, I suddenly feel petty and selfish with my decision to leave Roma High School, to leave my students on this very day when they need me most. I remember why I wanted to teach in the first place. It was never to become the principal, though I still believe I would have made a great one. No, it was to connect with the kids, especially the outsiders, to teach them the important lessons and share the wisdom that understanding our nation's history has to offer their developing minds. Today of all days, a teacher can make a difference in helping these young citizens understand what has happened, and perhaps provide some hope for better days ahead.

"Mr. Barrows, I'm sorry about the wait. They're calling an emergency School Board meeting tonight. We have to figure out how we're going to handle this Columbine school shooting with our students. Horrible what happened. We'll be offering special counseling sessions for any student who wants to talk. We're also going to have to take a look at school security around here. Right now, anyone can walk into this building. Anyway, what was it you wanted to talk about?"...

It took me a half hour to drive home from school, which is usually just a five-minute trip. Visibility was almost zero and the wind was taking down one tree after another as pelting rain saturated and softened the ground beneath the roots. Looking out my living room window from inside the house my parents built on Miller's End, I feel safe and secure as the storm waters flood our street and the neighborhood trees sway back and forth, refusing to surrender to the storm's vicious onslaught. In my meeting with Principal Turner, we never did talk about my leaving, or why I was passed over for principal, or why Sally Sutherland was chosen. Instead, we talked about the students, and how tomorrow was going to be a very important day at Roma High School...a day I very much wanted to be a part of, as their teacher.

GINO'S LAST HURRAH

They cancelled our Roma 10K in September of 2001 because of the World Trade Center bombings. I guess folks figured that following Saturday was just too damn soon after the 911 attacks to hold our annual race. People were either too depressed or too damned scared to run, was the thinking. But not everyone agreed, a few of us showed up anyway...

Most runners in Vermont, and a good many from much further away, know all about Roma's 10K, that's 6.2 miles in American. Our scenic course runs straight up and right back down Mount Mansfield, and is one of the few races that still serves beer at the finish line. I'm always amazed how enticing the promise of beer, that's free beer, is to runners over that last mile as we try to muster whatever passes for a strong finish these days. Maybe that's just me.

There's something magical about crossing that finish line, after running faster and further than anyone thought you could, that makes even Lite beer taste like honey nectar dripped down from the goddess Nike herself. Besides, when else do you get to drink a beer, or two, or three, with a clear conscience and a big smile at ten o'clock in the morning.

I've been running the Roma 10K for twenty-three years now. Some might call it a stretch to say what I do is running. I'm in my forties, so each year I get a little bit heavier and a whole lot slower. But I keep showing up every second weekend in September, lace up my hardly-ever-used running shoes, put out my best effort and always try to sprint past the finish line on Main Street, waving gallantly to the roaring Roma crowd. Then I collapse for the rest of the weekend. This year was different though; this race was personal.

It was the day before, on Friday, at his funeral, that I heard the race had been cancelled. I guess there were signs posted all over town, ads in the newspaper, even announcements on the radio and television stations. But as usual, I failed to get the message. No matter, I didn't care if it was cancelled, my mind was already made up. I was running. The night before, as I settled in for my ten- hour pre-race snooze after my carbo-load of spaghetti and meatballs, I knew this run was going to mean more than all the others combined. I didn't need anyone's permission, I knew the course by heart. It was really just up and down the mountain, with a few side trails thrown in for impact. I'd just get out there and do it. I'd run it for them. I'd run it for me. But most of all, I'd run it for him, for my dad, Gino Gallo.

He always showed up to watch me run this 10K from his usual spots around the course. Dad said it was the only time Roma people came out of their homes and actually spoke to each other, as they shared the moment watching us runners go by. It's going to seem strange not seeing his face in the crowd today, not hearing that deep bellowing voice cheering me on, calling out my name and promising to meet me at the finish line. Gino Gallo is no longer with us, and my world is already a much emptier place without him.

I'm one of the lucky ones because I knew him well. There's a line from an old Leonard Cohen song that says,"It's Father's Day and Everybody's Wounded"…not everybody; some of us sons got to know our fathers as the best friends we'd ever have in our lives. Too few really, as most guys I talk to never were close to their dads; all they can remember are violent outbursts and long bouts of silence. That makes it hard to get close, or even nearby. It seems like women are much better suited to be moms than men are to be dads. Moms are naturally better at communicating with kids. But my dad was the exception. Gino Gallo sure could talk about the things that mattered most in life.

I arrive this perfect Fall Saturday morning of race day 2001 after riding my bike through what could pass for a ghost town in an old Hollywood western. This scene is such a far cry from the usual throng of one-thousand-plus runners loosening up and doing pre-race wind sprints while music blares from giant speakers as the crowd gathers to witness the start. Today though, there are no signs of the beautiful small town life that comes so alive around Roma's little 10K.

I stash my bicycle behind the hedges fronting Roma's high school and go inside. An eerie silence hangs over the darkened gymnasium which is usually a madhouse scene as runners bounce from table to table in search of race numbers, T-shirts and giveaways. To my surprise there actually is one table staffed with stalwart volunteers handing out T-shirts for the race that never was. I grab an extra-large because they always shrink, and walk back outside to his usual pre-race perch. I am surprised to see a few more runners have arrived and are stretching in the early morning silence. Haven't they heard the Roma 10K is cancelled this year?

Nobody speaks. It's all very stoic as I watch everyone gather from my viewpoint beneath the giant elm that sits atop the rise overlooking our starting line. This was his spot. He'd wave to me and shout out, "Go get it, Frankie" with a coffee in one had and a jelly doughnut in the other, just before the starter's gun went off. It's a good spot. From here I can see the magical moment come together as more than a few runners converge from all directions, moving with a resigned purpose and a distinct silence to line up at the starting line for the 2001 Roma 10K, the race that never officially took place.

I feel humbled seeing the pride and focus on the faces of this disparate band of runners as we take our marks and wait in stillness for the race to begin. Each runner here today has decided for their own private reasons and personal beliefs that on this day, more important than any other, this race should be run. Tears well up in my eyes, tears I have been holding back far too long, tears I will have to hold back just a bit longer.

A few minutes before nine o'clock, two Roma police cars appear to escort our unsanctioned procession through the empty village streets, past the town hall, to begin our ascent up the mountain road. I look around and estimate there are maybe one hundred runners now. Chester Connelly, our local limousine driver who is wearing an old- school grey sweatsuit and black Converse high-top sneakers, walks to the front of our group and unfurls a weathered American flag. He hands it to one of the younger front runners and asks him to carry it forward. At precisely nine, a gun goes off, from where I don't know, and we begin our journey. I look up at that big elm tree in front of the school and I swear I can see him, coffee and jelly doughnut in hand. He's smiling at me and yells out, "Go get it, Frankie."

I don't really like to run, don't even consider myself a runner by any stretch of the imagination, mine or anyone else's. As we cover our first mile, I remember why. Running is a shock to the system–that's why. There's really no good reason to do this to your body. Why do I run at all if I hate it so much? I ask myself this same question the first couple of strides of this race every year. The answer is always the same—because this race brings out the best of Roma, our little not-so-perfect mountain town. Roma's 10K forces people to put aside their differences and act neighborly while sharing a genuine moment of togetherness. It's small-town Americana at its Rockwellian best. Anyone who wants to participate and run the distance is included, and cheered along the way by crowds of spectators from all walks of life. There's no elitism, no exclusion, just people wanting the best for each other, at least for the hour or so it takes to run and celebrate the race. You don't feel that kind of unity anymore, but you can always find that spirit alive and well at Roma's 10K, and every other small town race I've been to. That's really my only reason for ever running these races, to see people at their very best. I have noticed, once the race is over, that we-are-all-one feeling goes away just as quickly as the beer tent gets broken down.

As we run silently through the streets today there are no families lining the course with their children passing out water cups and spraying hoses to refresh us. We pass Reardon's General Store, just before the first mile marker, where Rufus and is dad, Rufus Senior would usually cut up oranges and hand them to us, as Rocky's fight theme and Chariots of Fire music set the mood for our trek up the mountain. Not today though, the store is dark and the Reardons are nowhere to be seen. We make the first mile at just over an eight-minute pace. For me, that's even a little fast. There are more than a few runners behind me, which makes me feel good. We stop and wait for them.

Without any discussion, it seems we have decided to run this race together, undivided as one. The alpha runners, those true striders whose long legs and zero body fat give them the look of cheetahs on the hunt, reach each mile marker first, then stop to wait for the rest of us less fleet-of-foot. I immediately love this strategy, understanding that today unity is so much more important than competition. We wait in silence for everyone to complete that first mile, then the lead runners take off again with Chester Connelly's flag waving proudly up front in the crisp September breeze.

I look over to where the bagpipe brigade usually plays and swear I see him walking up the hill. This was another of his favorite spots. He loved the bagpipe music and claimed Italy had invented the bagpipes, not Scotland. He even had a leather-bound history book he said proved it. I never did read that book, but I do still have it stacked somewhere.

Gino Gallo took spectating seriously. His generation was from a different time and place in this country, a world where attending an event just to witness and cheer was as significant as the players performing in it. He once told me about seeing Babe Ruth play at Yankee Stadium in the Sultan of Swat's latter years. He shared that story more than a few times, how even toward the end of his career when the Babe was so fat and could hardly run at all, opposing teams still respected his power and played him deep, just for insurance. Every so often, the Babe would lay down a bunt and the crowd would roar as the big man drove his three-hundred-plus pounds down the first base line just fast enough to beat the throw. My dad was there to see that happen, it was a keeper memory for Gino…"What is life anyway but a handful of moments worth remembering, Frankie?"

It's only mile two and I'm already tired. I remember that old Olympic commercial that began…"There is a hill in Kenya"…was that a beer commercial? I think it was. It showed this lean Kenyan, probably a famous runner at the time, who looked like a perfectly designed running machine. Sweat glistened on his sinewy aerodynamic body as he sprinted up what looked like more of a mountain than a hill somewhere in Kenya. There's also a hill in Roma...one that holds the same mythic challenge to us of lesser endurance, strength and speed. Every year, I run up this hill just a little bit slower, watching runners break stride and come to a complete stop, surrendering forever to Roma's cardiac hill. Not me though, not yet I am proud to say, and definitely not today. I've always understood that if I stop on this hill even once, I will never make it up without stopping again. Gino taught me that keeping stride, no matter how slow you go, is what matters most at this stage of the race. I see the faces around me as we slowly make our way up the hill. Everyone today is deep inside their own head, determined not to stop, to keep on moving forward no matter what.

We regroup at the two mile marker, or where it would have been. I arrive in the middle of our group. Looking down at the village of Roma, I am struck by how naturally beautiful our mountain haven is. Growing up here, and never really leaving for more than a few days, it's easy to forget the raw scenic wonder of where we live. Gino knew that. When I'd complain that our house wasn't big enough for our family and how it was falling apart, he'd say, "Forget about the house, Frankie. All houses fall apart, that's what they do. It's about the land, that's what matters most. We get to live here, Frankie."

There he is again, sitting on Overlook Rock where the water stop usually is. Here, he liked to hand me an empty water cup as I limped by after conquering that second mile.

"It's all uphill from here, Frankie." Yeah, he got a kick out of saying that every year.

I look around me at the determined faces pursuing our silent mission without official sanction. Just like the country we are trying to honor, this fleeting light brigade is made up of a tapestry of stories. Up ahead, Birdie Burkenstock, who runs the rental shop at the ski lodge, pushes Billy, her one-year-old son, in one of those three-wheeled running strollers. The kid is huge. He's already too big for the stroller; his legs and arms hang out, almost touching the ground as Birdie labors to push him up the mountain. I'll bet he weighs fifty pounds already. How can they still be ahead of me?

Ava Wagner, one of our neighbors over on Miller's End, runs by me wearing a photo of a fireman taped to her broad tanned back. I've known Ava ever since she was that little squirt of a kid in pigtails who lived three houses down, always riding her bike trying to catch up with me and her brother, Wally, as we disappeared into the woods to lose her. Now, she's that beautiful school teacher who every guy in town is trying to catch up with. Funny how things turn out. I wonder who that fire fighter is in her photo.

I see Cassie and Ollie Osborn together like always, running side-by-side in matching outfits of NYPD hats and sweatshirts. They've lived in Roma forever. Who did they know at the World Trade Center?

Three of the lead runners, two men and a Nordic-looking woman I don't know carry a green banner that reads, Cantor-Fitzgerald. They have that broker look to them, lean but maybe not so mean today. How many of their close friends and co-workers died in the World Trade Center attacks? It will be weeks, even months before anyone truly knows.

As we reach our halfway point, there are still no onlookers along the streets to bear witness to our silent procession commemorating this attack that changed everything. I'm starting to feel a bit like an imposter, as I am dedicating my race to him, before the others. Gino didn't die in the World Trade Center or in the line of duty. I don't even know if he'd ever been to the World Trade Center; most people haven't, and now they never will. Everyone else running today seems to know someone who was taken suddenly in those explosions heard and seen around the world. I can feel and understand their pain; I wonder if they can understand mine. For just this one moment, I believe they can.

We're moving faster now, slipping into a higher gear in our fourth mile. I am sure the leaders are slowing their usual pace drastically just to make sure we all stay together. I've managed to keep Chester's flag in sight for our entire journey. We stop briefly at the four mile marker. Everyone seems to be keeping up now, as if we're growing stronger. Usually this spot is a major hub of activity, with Cub Scouts and Little Leaguers passing out precious H2O to parched runners as we begin our home stretch. But today, all I see is a lone police car watching us pass by. Our group tightens now as the mountain road narrows coming down the utility route from the ski resort.

"It's all downhill from here, Frankie. See you at the finish. First beer's on me, kid." I can hear his voice but see no one standing in his usual spot. Why can't I see you, Gino?

We stop as a group at five miles, making that last mile stretch in just under eight minutes, a personal record for me at this stage of the race. Most of us are breathing heavy now, but it doesn't matter because we all know there's only that one last mile to go. I don't want this race to end now. If we keep on running, maybe things will get better again and all the pain will go away.

Before we begin our final mile home, one of the alpha runners, the one who carried Chester's flag, says he believes we should symbolize our effort today to honor those who died at the World Trade Center. Did anyone have any ideas? These were the first words spoken during our entire run. After what seemed like a long silence, Birdie Burkenstock suggests we each pick up a stone, one for each person remembered, and place them beneath the flagpole in the park by the school. Little Ivan, who graduated from Roma High School just a few years ago and lives in Boston now, says we should stop in front of the firehouse and sing "America the Beautiful." Normally, Ivan's idea would seem corny to me but today, in this moment, it seems just right. I find a smooth alabaster rock with a solid streak of red running down the center, and fall in behind our tattered flag. Without uttering another word, we are moving again as one. We are in the final mile of the race that never was, Roma's 10K of 2001.

Maybe I save too much for the end, but the homestretch is always easy for me. I like to finish strong. That's my race strategy, start weak and finish strong. I'll usually sprint down Main Street past the firehouse and Grady's Pub trying to shave off a precious minute from my finishing time. Not today though, my bond with this group is much too strong for personal gain. We have all started this journey together and stayed united throughout so righteously, we should finish as one.

We gather in front of the firehouse and sing "America the Beautiful," paying tribute to the men and women who lost their lives trying to save others on September 11th. Then we gather at the flagpole and one by one name the people we each want to honor, carefully placing our stones at the base of the flag. The sun shines bright over a cloudless blue sky, while a crisp wind blowing down from the mountain billows the flag as our last stones are laid to rest.

We stand in silence for the next few minutes, each one of us lost deep in thought for the people in our lives who matter so much that we showed up here today. It seems as if nobody wants to leave. Slowly though, people begin to peel away and walk silently into the different directions their lives will take them. I am the last person to leave the scene. The park is empty now, resoundingly still. I look for him one last time, and I see Gino clear as this day has become, standing in front of Grady's Pub, motioning me to come over and have one more beer with him before we head home, just like we always did. We smile at each other, then my dad, Gino Gallo, is gone, taking one final keeper moment with him for his journey onward.

When I placed my stone beneath the flag, I declared proudly my reason for running...

"I'm here today for Eugene "Gino" Gallo, Roma's retired police chief. He was born June 22nd, 1919 and died September 10th, 2001 just hours before the world he knew and understood was drastically and violently changed forever. Gino Gallo was a World War II hero, he was my dad and he never missed a Roma 10K. He's still here today, cheering for us every step of the way. Thank You, Gino, for everything...I miss you already, dad.

September 11, 2001—CNN REPORTS ON EVENTS OF 911—

Nineteen men hijacked four fuel-loaded US commercial airplanes bound for West Coast destinations. A total of 2,977 people were killed in New York City, Washington DC and Shanksville, Pennsylvania. The attack was orchestrated by al Qaeda leader Osama bin Laden.

At the World Trade Center site in Lower Manhattan, 2763 people were killed when hijacked American Airlines Flight 11 and United Airlines Flight 175 were intentionally crashed into the north and south towers, or as a result of the crash. Of those who perished from the initial attacks and the subsequent collapses of the towers, 343 were New York City firefighters, 23 were New York City police officers and 37 were officers of the Port Authority. The victims ranged in age from two to eighty-five years.

At the Pentagon in Washington DC, 184 people were killed when hijacked American Airlines Flight 77 crashed into the building.

Near Shanksville, Pennsylvania 40 passengers and crew members aboard United Airlines Flight 93 died when the plane crashed into a field...

BANKER TAKES A HOLIDAY

He won't be in today, or tomorrow, or the day after that. Peter Wellington has left the building and he won't be coming back. I knew this day was coming…

Peter Wellington's been the Chief Investment Officer of New England Savings and Loan for more than twenty years. He's made a lot of money for the bank with his unconventional investment bets. Peter's also been skimming money from some of our largest account holders and pension funds. I've been watching, some might say even helping him do it these last few years.

"Excuse me, Monique, are we having our meeting today?"

"Yes, Stella, I'll be out in just a few minutes. Mr. Wellington is on extended holiday starting today, so I'll be running things until he gets back. We'll meet in the conference room at nine-thirty."

"Wow, that was sudden. He didn't say anything last week. Where did he go?"

"I'm not sure where, but I'm sure it's an island with a white sandy beach and lots of rum drinks. You know how Mr. Wellington is about his vacation getaways, very secretive, lots of photos after but all hush-hush before he goes. Tell Max and Skyler we'll meet in ten minutes."

We're just a small branch with only the five of us staffing it. Peter insisted on being based here in Roma where he owns a ski chalet, which makes us a very important branch. As Chief Investment Officer, Peter personally looks after the accounts of our most affluent customers and handles all the corporate and government investments. Working together these last ten years we've become a highly functional family here at Roma's Savings and Loan. Stella is our newest addition. She joined us almost four years ago but we still call her the 'newbie'. I've been the Managing Director and Peter's right hand man, so to speak, since he set up shop here in Roma. Max and Skyler joined us right out of college as tellers, which they basically still are as there's really no other positions to rise to in a branch this small. We enjoy each other. It's rare when you look forward to arriving at work just to see the people you work with. I don't want that to change. But sometimes change is for the best.

****

BALI, INDONESIA

Somebody's got to be the fall guy if you're going to take a lot of money. I saw my moment and I took it. Everything's falling apart because the people at the very top got too greedy. A little greed is okay. Hell, that's what capitalism is set up to reward. But too much greed will kill the golden pig every time.

"Would you like another Bintang sir?"

"Why yes, I believe another Bintang beer is in order. And what is that couple over there drinking with the umbrella in it?"

"That is an Arak Attack, sir, chilled Balinese white wine mixed with coconut and rum. Very potent."

"Yes, I believe I'll have one of those as well, with another Bintang. What time is the next ferry to Jakarta?"

"Next ferry at noon, in one hour sir."

"Better yet, where can I buy a boat around here, a motor boat?"

"There's a boat yard down the shore road, about a mile from here. They sell motorboats, fishing boats and jet skis too."

"Fantastic, why take the ferry when I can motorboat to Jakarta myself. I'm looking forward to my first Arak Attack."

Monique understood the game all along. With all those late nights working together, how could we not end up in bed. I have to hand it to her though, she played me like a fiddle, never saw her coming. The apprentice outplays the master. But like I always say, if you have to lose, let it be to a woman. They belong on top. Monique can handle everything back at the branch while I fish the Indian Ocean and get to know these islands. What's my new name? I keep forgetting. Oh yeah, it's Patrick Parnell, the perfect name for a retired banker, now a beachcomber in training. Finally I get to play that crazy Irishman who wakes up every day ready for a new adventure without a care in the world. In Bali no less.

You can't escape the bad news though, even down here in the middle of the bluest ocean ever. I can hear the television in the bar reporting how the U.S. markets are imploding, the S&P's down another ten percent dipping below a thousand for the first time in years. Bernanke's Fed is begging the Treasury to keep printing money to hand over to the banks who started this whole mess in the first place. Trillions of dollars are being moved and laundered and handed out just to prop up the stock market and save our capitalist way of life at the highest levels of society. Who says we don't want socialism in the US of A? We already have it working well for the ultra-rich and the too big to fail. That's why I did what I did, I recognized the moment for what it was. It will be a long while before they even notice the few million that's gone missing from my portfolio. With a little luck of the Irish, they may never notice. Monique can make sure of that.

"Your Bintang, sir, and the Arak Attack. I put in an extra umbrella for good luck and a soft landing."

"Oh, I am excited. My first Arak Attack with an extra umbrella even. What did you say your name was?"

"I didn't say, sir, but it's Diah."

"Beautiful name, what does it mean? I'm sure it has an exotic meaning. Everything and everyone is exotic in Bali, Diah."

"You funny. Diah means powerful woman, sir."

"Enough with the sirs, call me Patrick. Your name fits you, Diah."

****

ROMA, VERMONT

"Mr. Wellington has gone on an extended holiday. He left instructions for us to carry on as if he was here. He'll check in with me to answer any questions that may arise. If anyone asks for Mr. Wellington, just say he is on holiday. If they press further or if it seems urgent, please refer them to me."

"Is everything alright with him? It seems so sudden and he didn't say anything about being gone last week."

"Yes, Max, it was a quick decision. He mentioned it to me and he was out on Thursday and Friday. But he seemed fine and happy about his trip."

"When is he due back?"

"I'm not sure of the exact date, Stella. He was unclear about that, and he does have plenty of vacation time built up, well over a month, I believe.

"Should we forward all of his calls to you, Monique? What about his meetings that are already scheduled?"

"Yes, Skylar, good point, as always. I'll take his calls. Go ahead and print me out his meeting schedule for the next month. I'll reschedule them, or if they insist on getting together, I'll take the meeting. The plan is, we will continue working as a team just as if Mr. Wellington was still here. Now, let's all get into place. We still have a bank to run and customers to serve."

Their faces look confused as they leave the conference room. Peter always keeps everyone focused and everything moving in our small branch that has become so important because of him. Without Peter here using Roma as his base of operations, corporate will probably close us down. The longer he officially stays on holiday, the better for everyone.

****

BALI, INDONESIA

The people are all so beautiful here with an innocence and purity that we've long lost. This is the paradise everyone dreams about but very few ever actually get to experience. Indonesia is thousands of sun-drenched little islands with white sandy beaches that stretch into the warm and gentle waves of the Indian Ocean. A man could easily get lost down here, lose his way in the bare-breasted brown skinned Diahs strolling the beaches, so free-spirited and unaware of their natural beauty. What's my rush, Jakarta's banks can wait.

Seems like a better idea to spend more time right here in Bali. Maybe Diah can show me around and help me find a boat, sturdy and reliable enough to explore these islands. She did give me that extra umbrella. What day is it anyway, Tuesday or Wednesday maybe? Time means nothing here to these people, to this place where statues, temples and fountains date back thousands of years. We take ourselves so seriously with our meetings and billable hours and daily planners, when it's really happiness and tranquility in the moment that matter most. Of course, even a little bit money can go a long way down here as you're searching for that inner peace.

****

ROMA, VERMONT

He hadn't left me a note or told me anything at all about his plans for departure. I just knew it was time for Peter to go. The signs were all there. He had used ten million of the twenty-five million dollars in TARP money to pay back the accounts he had been skimming from over these past years. Smart move, erase the old theft to create the new one. That left roughly fifteen-million dollars to invest into bond and security funds, where he should have placed the money in the first place. The good news was, by not investing it he hadn't suffered the staggering losses all those other banks had. Just coming out at breakeven would be considered a major victory during these dark market days.

As Chief Investment Officer for our bank, Peter has full discretion on all investment decisions. In reality, he answers to nobody because no one else fully understands what he is doing. They only care about the results that make them look good, so they continue to leave Peter alone.

I followed Peter's money trail to see where he placed the remaining fifteen million dollars. He put five million into some highly speculative technology funds focused on social media and cyber-security, then placed the remaining ten million dollars into a general fund he named 'Beachcomber'. Eureka! This was the account I monitored and gained access to over these last few weeks. It was Peter's escape hatch; then it was only a matter of figuring when he was going to use it to climb out of Roma.

It was a search I found on his computer last month that pushed me to do it. Peter had been looking into flight schedules to the Bahamas and the Cayman Islands, innocent enough in itself, but both are well known off-shore banking safe havens. He was ready to make his move. I knew it because I know Peter Wellington like nobody else does. Peter is a master at moving money to the right place at the right time, which is what has made him so successful with the bank's investments for so long. Everyone wants Peter Wellington to be personally involved with their investments, and once again Peter had not let them down. He gave them a break-even when everyone else had lost everything. Peter had covered his gambling losses and left just enough of the TARP money to make his getaway and fund his retirement in style. He had thought of everything. But he forgot about me.

In our many long nights and weekends of working and playing together, Peter had told me more than once, nobody really needs more than five-million dollars to live a carefree, comfortable and happy life.

"Anything beyond five million is pure greed," according to Peter.

If you invested the five million wisely and safely, you could live off the interest to the tune of two-hundred-thousand plus dollars a year and never have to touch the original five million. That's what the old money does with much higher amounts; they never touch the principal and only spend the interest. He said it so many times I stored it in memory and took it from his bank. That's exactly where I capped him, moving five-million dollars out of his 'Beachcomber' fund and placed it in an account I set up called the 'Rainbow' fund, for the pot of gold it held within. As it turned out, I moved the five-million just days before Peter made his great escape. That's the other valuable lesson Peter Wellington taught me, the importance of timing. He taught me well.

****

BALI, INDONESIA

I watch the noon ferry leave for Jakarta as I down my second Arak Attack. The mixture of rum, coconut juice and rice wine turns the drink into a potent punch. Not having slept for three days makes me even more susceptible to its intoxicating powers. With each sip I feel completely relaxed, reborn even.

Bali is far too beautiful an island to leave in a rush for the big, busy city of Jakarta. After three days of flying, with brief stops in Grand Cayman and the Bahamas to open up accounts and establish new credit lines, I need at least a week to rejuvenate. That final hop from Singapore to Bali on

Indonesian Air Garuda was a bumpy ride the whole way. At one point, I thought we were going down into the Indian Ocean, but apparently they always fly that low to save on fuel. Waves were hitting the plane. I could see the big fish getting ready to eat me.

I still can't figure out how Monique conjured up my password to gain access into 'Beachcomber'. I guess if anyone was going to get in, it had to be Monique. After all, it was our safeword. She's quite the force of nature, that Monique. But five million? What's she going to do with five-million dollars in Roma without getting noticed?

"Well hello, Diah, I thought you were never coming back. Is that Arak Attack for me? Three umbrellas this time. You're starting to like me, Diah, I can tell."

"Of course I come back. You, my only customer now. That other couple went back to their room. Arak Attack makes you want to take a long nap."

"I'm feeling kind of tired myself. Still a bit parched though. I was wondering, Diah, since I'm new to Bali and you're not, maybe you could show me around and help me find the Lagoon Hotel. What time do you get off?"

"I usually leave after lunchtime. The hotel is that one, right there on the lagoon. I could walk with you over there and introduce you to the owner. He also owns the boatyard, so you can ask him about your motorboat and maybe a jet ski. Everyone likes the jet ski to get around Bali."

"What's my name?"

"Patrick. It is a good name. What does it mean?"

"Yes, I like my name, that's why I chose it. I believe it means hero of Ireland. Looks like I'm going to be eating some lunch, Diah. What smells so delicious? Bring me some of whatever I smell and definitely another Bintang. I'm hungry and thirsty for a new life, Diah. But let's start with lunch."

"You smell Babi Guling, the roasted pig. You should also try the fresh grilled fish and our spicy Sambal Seafood with some Nasi Goreng, fried rice. Then you will take a long nap at the Lagoon Hotel. I'll come by later tonight and show you around town."

"Bring on the food, Diah. I'm already loving Bali. I'll eat, I'll sleep and then we'll be merry."

"You funny, Patrick."

"Yes I am funny, Diah, and I'm just getting warmed up."

****

ROMA, VERMONT

I won't tell them until everything settles down. Stella, Max and Skyler each now own one million dollars worth of shares in Case-Morgain, the bank that started this global financial disaster in the first place, so of course it will come through this crisis the healthiest. If you light the fuse you know when the bomb is going to explode before everyone else does. If anyone's too big to fail, it is Case-Morgain. They're already using all that TARP money the government gave them to buy back their own stock instead of making loans to people who need them. Like Peter always said, "Greed only gets greedier." In five years or so, their one million dollars of stock should

110

double or triple, maybe even quadruple if they leave it alone and let the government prop up the market to new all-time highs in the name of preaching Capitalism to the rest of the world. "Once you understand the game, predicting the future is easy." That was another one of Peter's many sayings.

I would have loved to have seen his face when he made that first deposit down in the Caymans, minus the five million. It only took me seven tries to figure out his password, our safeword...SURRENDER. How many times did I hear him say it? Peter always talked about Bali, his paradise on earth. He had visited there in college on his Semester At Sea, the WASP version of a walkabout. I'm pretty sure Indonesia is where he'll disappear to. It's where I'll go looking for him when the time is right and the coast is clear. SURRENDER, Peter, I'll find you...

—2008 ECONOMIC COLLAPSE REPORTED BY CNN ECONOMIC NEWS—

The 2008 Financial Crisis is considered by many economists to have been the most serious financial crisis since the Great Depression of the 1930's. Under Republican President George W. Bush, the financial crisis began in 2007 with the collapse of the deregulated subprime home mortgage market in the United States, and then developed into a full blown international banking crisis by September of 2008. Massive bailouts totaling more than 400 billion dollars to prevent financial collapse of the world financial system were given to banks and financial institutions that had made reckless bets and bad investments. Under TARP (Troubled Asset Relief Program) the Treasury Department provided 400 plus billion dollars to inject capital into the failing banks and other too big to fail institutions. Most banks used the TARP money to buy back their own stock at the lowest market price instead of making loans to their customers in dire need who had been impacted by the crisis. Now, more than ten years later, billions of dollars given to the banks under TARP remain unaccounted for and may never be recovered.

OLD MAN MILLER

We all live in different worlds...my world is different from your world, is different from her world, so different from his world. Sure, we share the same planet but no two of our journeys are quite the same. While our paths may cross briefly, we are ultimately alone in our world, solitary on our journey through this life. It is only the very few people who we let into our lives to share those precious moments of love, joy, happiness, romance, adventure...these people make each of our worlds better places to be, if only for a moment.

I watch all the worlds on Miller's End pass by from right here on my front porch. You've probably seen me in your own neighborhood. I'm that old guy, always sitting on his porch no matter what the season or how harsh the weather. You wave to me or say hello as you go by my house, but you don't really know or even care to know anything about me. I've just been in the neighborhood longer than anyone can remember and will be here even longer after everyone leaves. My world is the oldest of everyone's; these people, my neighbors here on Miller's End, are shooting stars passing me by, as their journeys cross fleetingly into my world then disappear forever into the vast galaxies beyond.

The Millers purchased this farmland back in 1860, just before the Civil War broke out. Their 100-acre farm stretched halfway up the mountainside on the sun-drenched south-facing slope. Mathius and Hattie Miller had a real love for their land and the rich, fertile soil they planted. They were true farmers, and this was a working farm with acres of hay, barley and corn harvested to provide for Roma and the neighboring towns. They kept horses, cows, chickens and pigs right here on these twenty-five front acres that today are called Miller's End.

This house, my home since forever, was their original farmhouse. I grew up in this house and never left; there are far too many memories here to just up and leave behind.

It was their son, Lucius Miller, who decided to sell the land to a developer from Boston who planned on building one-hundred Roma homes, each unique in design and each set on a one-acre plot, stretching all the way up the mountain's south slope. Then the Depression hit. Like most builders, the developer ran out of money and ended up only constructing ten of the one-hundred homes envisioned. These are the homes of my neighbors who live here with me. Lucius insisted on naming the street Miller's End, as sadly, it marked the end of the Millers as Vermont farmers. In selling the land just before the Great Depression, Lucius Miller made what was considered a great deal of money back then, but he never did forgive himself for selling the family farm.

Today, Miller's End is a hidden right-hand turn that's easy to miss if you're not looking for it, located half-way up the mountain road and only a ten-minute walk from downtown Roma. My front porch looks out on the entire neighborhood and let's me see all those who pass through my world.

"Hello, Mr. Miller. Nice day today."

"Supposed to thunder later, Wally. Better get those newspapers delivered early or you're gonna get drenched in the storm."

Wally Wagner never did stop delivering the news. He went on to the university in Burlington and studied journalism. He started out as a small-town newspaper reporter covering everything from pie-eating contests to local election results.

114

Then after a few years, Wally got hired by CNN to report the news on television. He travelled all over the world covering wars, riots, famine and corruption before he finally came back home to Roma where he always belonged. Wally's the editor, publisher and owner of our little Roma Gazette, back to reporting the real news about spelling bees, little league championships and town meeting arguments. It's funny how life takes you full circle if you let it, if you just keep moving forward and follow the signs. Wally Wagner reported the news from more than fifty countries, only to find out the stories that really mattered were the ones happening right here in Roma.

My next-door neighbor to the right over here is Principal Barrows. That's right, he decided to keep teaching and a few years later when Sally Sutherland was fired for playing steal the bacon with the gym teacher, they needed a new principal in a hurry.

Mr. Barrows was the ideal choice for principal, he always had been. The students loved Principal Barrows, the parents not so much. When a bunch of moms decided to fire the basketball coach and cancel the season because a new girl in Roma was getting all the credit and stealing all the headlines for a rare winning season, Principal Barrows decided enough was enough. After serving fifteen years as principal of Roma High School he walked out, and this time he didn't look back. He just up and left on a rainy April afternoon. I recollect it was on the 20th of April.

Principal Barrows doesn't have much to do with the school anymore. Once in a while you'll see him watching a soccer or field hockey game from the hill overlooking the playing fields; mostly though, he just stays away and keeps to himself. Roma High School has gone steadily down that hill of decline since the day he quit. Without a principal who looked out for the students, there was no one to stop the parents from turning the school into their own private playground, trying to relive those high school moments that never worked out for them the first time around. We wave at each other, but Principal Barrows never says much anymore. Those parents stole his joy.

At the end of the street, just before where the woods start, that's Otis Oleger's house. People say it's haunted because of the lights turning on and off and the bells clanging in the middle of the night, but that's just Otis and Elizabeth moving things around. They're still getting settled in after all these years. Otis and Elizabeth like to take their daily stroll around the neighborhood at dusk and hike into the woods all the way up to the summit on full moon nights. I always give them a wave and make a choo-choo sound when I see them coming. It makes Otis smile. Some folks say they see Otis riding the trains to Burlington, or Boston, or Albany. But that can't be right. Otis died in his sleep that very night after he rode the last train to Roma. He's still wearing his conductor uniform every time I see him, walking hand in hand with Elizabeth Engel, his childhood sweetheart, the both of them so very happy to be back together.

The Gallo family live just across the street on the corner, by the Mountain Road turnoff. Gino was Roma's police chief for a bunch of years, and they were good years. He died the day before the September 11th attack on the World Trade Center towers. It was a gunshot wound from World War II that finally got him. Turns out they didn't remove all the bullets from his fight with the Japanese holdouts when he was trying to get out of that cave in the Philippines. One bullet landed too close to his heart to get at safely so they left it in there. Every year when they checked him out at the Veterans Hospital, the bullet had inched just a little bit closer to his aorta, until one day it punctured right through. I saw it happen; he was over there mowing his front lawn. Gino gave me a wave and I saluted him back, just like always. He stood there at attention for a few seconds with a funny look on his face, then he dropped backward onto his driveway. His lawnmower kept moving on down the street and across the Mountain Road before it finally stopped. Gino, dying the day before those 911 attacks happened was poetic justice to me—the world he knew and understood still existed, then the very next day it didn't. Gino believed right to the end that World War II was fought and won to make the world, everyone's world, a safer place and make sure this country was never attacked again. Gino Gallo was a true hero who lived each and every day for his family, always knowing that Japanese bullet was creeping closer and closer to its mark. His wife, Greta, died in her sleep a year to the day after Gino.

The Gallo kids all grew up and moved away from Roma, except for the oldest, Frankie, who delivers the mail around town. Ernest and Julio, the twins, became Navy Seals, and both won medals during the first Gulf War. Theresa taught economics at the university and became the school's first woman dean. But it was Gemma, the little girl who used to stargaze with Gino every night, who surprised everyone. Dr. Gemma Gallo is still reaching for those stars, working as a rocket scientist designing deep space satellites for a top secret company somewhere up there in Northern California.

Across the street from the Gallos, on the corner is the Stringer home. Sammy and his older brother, Sonny, still share all of Roma's athletic records in football, basketball, baseball, track and any other sport you can think of. I used to watch Sammy swinging that big Mickey Mantle bat on his front lawn for hours trying to perfect his home run swing. I'd always yell over, "Strike Three," then he'd look down the street at me, point up toward the sun and take a big swing, and yell back, "It's outta here, Mr. Miller." I guess he was right, it was out of here. Sammy Stringer made it all the way to the big leagues, winning two World Series championships with the Boston Red Sox, playing shortstop and smacking home runs, three of them game winners.

Rhonda and Tad finally did get married after running back and forth between homes for all those years. They each kept their own house, even after they tied the knot. Rhonda told me that separate bathrooms in separate houses were the keys to a long and happy marriage. Tad kept on taking his birdwatching hikes right up until the very day the country legalized marijuana. Suddenly, Tad wasn't so interested in the birds anymore but got busy turning his and Rhonda's backyards into a marijuana farm cultivating his Roma Budd, which quickly became a crowd favorite all over New England. I was just happy to see my parent's land being cultivated again.

Rhonda kept working at Grady's Happy Hour, serving her loyal customers four days a week. She also started a massage therapy business on the side, visiting the homes and offices of just about every rich and powerful person you can think of in Roma, the entire state of Vermont and all over New England. That must be one great massage Rhonda gives based on all the money she rakes in to pay for those trips she takes with Tad. They've traveled all over the world, those two. Rhonda's become quite the real estate mogul in Roma too; she owns everything downtown. That Tad's one lucky birdwatcher.

Monique Marlowe, my neighbor over to the left here, always gave me a big hello on her morning walk down Mountain Road to the bank, and a "good evening Mr. Miller" on her way home. Didn't matter the weather—rain, snow, sleet or hail—Monique always hiked into town. They promoted Monique to Chief Investment Officer at the Savings and Loan after her boss, Peter Wellington, left for a holiday and never came back, not even leaving a letter of resignation. It was just after that big financial crisis when he went missing. It took almost a year before the bank finally accepted that Peter wasn't coming back and might even be dead. By then, Monique had been managing all of Peter's clients and making investments in some tech stocks that paid off big. The bank decided to forget about Peter Wellington, and put its money on Monique. They let her run things right out of our Roma branch. Funny thing though, just a few years later, must have been two years, Monique went on her own banker's holiday and never came back. After she went missing, they ended up closing the Roma branch of Vermont Savings and Loan. They must have given some pretty nice severance packages to the folks working there, based on the cars and homes they all bought after getting laid off.

I sit here on my front porch and watch all of my friends and neighbors, each one their own world, shooting across my horizon. So many years later now, I see them just as they were—the loud, crazy Gallo kids running all over the neighborhood and across everyone's yards...rugged Monique strutting by, giving me a big wave on her walk to and from the bank...little Sammy Stringer swinging his oversized Mickey

Mantle and Hank Aaron bats at phantom pitches for hours in his front yard...they're all still here on Miller's End, just as I remember them, and they me. It's dusk now, that fleeting moment of transition when daylight fades to evening, then darkens to night. There's Otis and Elizabeth walking hand in hand just like always, right on time for their moonlight hike. I wave over to Principal Barrows who is planting tulips in his front yard as the rain starts to fall. Wally Wagner rides by, slowing down his bicycle just long enough to toss my newspaper onto the porch.

"You were right, Mr. Miller. It was gonna rain today. See you tomorrow."

"And tomorrow, and tomorrow and the next day too, Wally Wagner."

Down the street I can see Rhonda and Tad scurrying between their two houses putting all the garden tools away before the rain gets heavier and turns into a thunderstorm, like it always does here in Roma. Tad is still wearing that ridiculous pith helmet he always had on for his birdwatching hikes and Rhonda is wearing practically nothing at all, just like always. She sees me watching and blows me a kiss. I blow one back and make a bird call to Tad..."Chickadee, Chickadee."

But what about the Jimmies? I can't forget the two little goons over there across the street throwing rotten apples at each other. Jimmy DiGeorgino fell from his roof one April night and broke his pelvis. Nobody ever could figure out what he was doing up there on his roof with a loaded rifle and a night scope; he sure wasn't telling. I watched him fall that night, right here from my front porch. That ended any chance of him signing up for the Marines. He took a job working as a cop over there in Babylon and became friends with Conrad and

Satchmo, those two juvenile delinquent arsonists who burned down our town-hall belfry.

Jimmy Jackman's world took him far from Miller's End, all the way to Vietnam. His number came up in the lottery and he was drafted into the Marines where he learned how to fly helicopters. Captain Jimmy Jackman flew over one hundred combat missions and won a Bronze Star for bravery, a Purple Heart for getting wounded in action and the big one, a Congressional Medal of Honor. During the fall of Saigon, Captain Jimmy made twenty-five trips, flying both large and small helicopters, making dangerous rooftop landings to pick up hundreds of people who were desperate to escape Saigon before it fell to the North Vietnamese. He delivered them to safety and freedom aboard the U.S. Navy Ships waiting five miles out in the South China Sea. That's Captain Jimmy flying his helicopter in that famous rooftop photo taken during the evacuation. Later that same night, he made the final nighttime rescue of the remaining U.S. Marines from the rooftop of the CIA building to end Operation Frequent Wind. For his unselfish acts of heroism over that two-day mission, Captain Jimmy Jackman was awarded the Congressional Medal of Honor. Strange how Jimmy Jackman ended up doing everything in the Marines that Jimmy DiGeorgino wanted to do. I can still see them in their yards, throwing rotten apples at each other for hours.

She doesn't look as good as she used to, that's for sure. But if you drive the Mountain Road, about halfway up on your right you just might notice a weathered sign mostly covered nowadays by moss and tree limbs. But that sign still says, Miller's End. If you walk down that forgotten rocky road you'll come into my world, a neighborhood of once-happy homes filled with moments and stories of the people who passed through and never really left my front porch view. When you see me, Lucius Miller, why not pause for a moment to give a wave and say hello to that old man of the neighborhood who has always been there and always will be, sitting on his front porch watching and remembering all those worlds who passed by on their long journeys home.

...L'Chaim Baby, L'Chaim...

Childhood was all daydreams and play,
The teens just one long bad day;
My 20s was wild, My 30s much less,
Those 40s brought smiles, But 50s the best;
My 60s marched slowly toward 70s forced calm,
Now these silent night 80s embrace me,
Whispering 'time to move on'.
Born to this moment let infant begin,
This journey called Life,
Your own bumpy ride to our unfinished end.

...To Life Baby, To Life...

-YUP-

www.ingramcontent.com/pod-product-compliance
Lightning Source LLC
Chambersburg PA
CBHW070309280626
47159CB00018B/3328